MADE IN ACAPULCO

The Detective Emilia Cruz Stories

Carmen Amato

Published 2023 by Laurel & Croton (second edition)
ISBN: 979-8-9885363-9-0 (print)
ISBN 978-0-9853256-4-0 (ebook)

Praise for Detective Emilia Cruz

CLIFF DIVER

"From the moment I started the first one, I couldn't put it down. . . Her work touches on important issues affecting Mexico in a real, human way and is exciting, fast paced and utterly gripping." – *Mexico Retold*

HAT DANCE

[Emilia] is a force to be reckoned with." – *Mystery Sequels*

DIABLO NIGHTS

"Amato brings her characters to life with her vivid writing style and sets them on the streets of a Mexico steeped in Catholicism and corruption." – *OnlineBookClub.org*

KING PESO

"Danger and betrayal never more than a few pages away." – *Kirkus Reviews*

PACIFIC REAPER

"Carmen Amato . . . out does many of the best crime authors out there." – *Artisan Book Reviews*

43 MISSING

"A fast-paced procedural . . . a real page-turner . . . a very original plot." – *The BookLife Prize*

Also by Carmen Amato

DETECTIVE EMILIA CRUZ SERIES
CLIFF DIVER: Detective Emilia Cruz Book 1
HAT DANCE: Detective Emilia Cruz Book 2
DIABLO NIGHTS: Detective Emilia Cruz Book 3
KING PESO: Detective Emilia Cruz Book 4
PACIFIC REAPER: Detective Emilia Cruz Book 5
43 MISSING: Detective Emilia Cruz Book 6
RUSSIAN MOJITO: Detective Emilia Cruz Book 7
NARCO NOIR: Detective Emilia Cruz Book 8
MADE IN ACAPULCO: The Emilia Cruz Stories
THE ARTIST/EL ARTISTA: A Bilingual Short Story
FELIZ NAVIDAD FROM ACAPULCO: A Detective Emilia Cruz Novella
THE LISTMAKER OF ACAPULCO: A Detective Emilia Cruz Novella

GALLIANO CLUB SERIES
ROAD TO THE GALLIANO CLUB: Prequel
MURDER AT THE GALLIANO CLUB: Book 1
BLACKMAIL AT THE GALLIANO CLUB: Book 2
REVENGE AT THE GALLIANO CLUB: Book 3

THRILLERS
AWAKENING MACBETH
THE HIDDEN LIGHT OF MEXICO CITY

FOREWORD

The character of Emilia Cruz came to me after an encounter with a junkie in a church in Mexico City.

We were celebrating midnight Mass on Christmas Eve at Saint Patrick's Roman Catholic Church. A junkie armed with a handgun burst into the church, shouting and jerking as he staggered up the aisle toward the altar. The congregation froze.

I was in the first pew with my daughter and mother who was visiting from New York. My son, then 9 years old, was an altar server assisting our pastor, Father Richard Junius.

I recall thinking that as president of the parish council, it was my responsibility to do something. Perhaps I thought I could talk the guy down.

Waving his gun, the junkie demanded money. Father Richard dug through his robes to find a pocket and gave him a few pesos.

Distracted by the coins, the junkie allowed himself to be seized by several members of the congregation. The handgun was confiscated and the junkie led out of the church.

Mass resumed.

Neither my son nor my daughter remembers the episode.

Detective Emilia Cruz emerged from that encounter fully formed, conjured from the stress of the moment and the realization of how the drug war impacts Mexico.

I placed her in Acapulco not only because it is one of my

favorite places, with a name that instantly conjures up visions of beaches and nightclubs, but also because Acapulco is now one of the most violent cities in the Western Hemisphere. Drug cartels fight over points of entry and routes to lucrative markets in the United States.

Emilia Cruz is the first and only female police detective in Acapulco. She's a good liar, a fast thinker, and a mean kickboxer in a department that didn't want her and is still trying to break her. Even as she fights to keep what she's earned, Emilia keeps a record of women who have gone missing--casualties of Mexico's current chaos--and is always searching for *Las Perdidas*, the Lost Ones.

Now eight novels into the series, readers have embraced Emilia, recognizing that there is more to her story than drug war violence and official corruption. Emilia represents hope for Mexico, with its rich and diverse cultural heritage, beautiful landscapes and architecture, and of course, glorious food.

Carmen Amato
Wilson County, Tennessee

P.S. After the stories, enjoy an excerpt from political thriller THE HIDDEN LIGHT OF MEXICO CITY, longlisted for the 2020 Millennium Book Award.

Glossary of Spanish Terms

Abarrotes: snacks

Barrio: local neighborhood

Borracho: a drunk

Chica: girl

El Norte: the United States

El teniente: lieutenant

Halcone: word meaning falcon used by drug gangs to mean a person acting as a lookout

Jefe: chief, person in charge

Madre de Dios: Mother of God, used as exclamation

Mercado: market

Narcomanta: usually an oversized cloth banner, emblazoned with a message from a drug cartel

Norteamericano: North American

Pendejo: asshole, jerk

Placas: license plates

Pollo: chicken

Prima: cousin (female)

Privada: enclosed subdivision and/or the gate to the property

Rayos: exclamation, similar to "oh hell"

Sicario: cartel henchman or assassin

Turistas: tourists

Vaya con Dios: Go with God

Of note

Regarding Mexican names: It is the custom in Mexico to use two surnames. The first is from the father's family and is always used. The second surname is the name of the mother's father. The second is sometimes dropped in conversation and/or to shorten the name in keeping with American and European naming conventions.

Conversion rate: For the purposes of this novel, $1.00 = 10 Mexican pesos.

It is in one's work that we discover love and faith.

Mexican proverb

THE BEAST

Her opponent's flailing hand connected with the bridge of her nose and Emilia Cruz Encinos heard the snap before she felt the pain. Her eyes watered and her muscles screamed as she twisted far enough to protect her face by pushing it into the mat.

Montez was at least 20 kilos heavier than Emilia but he carried too much of it in his middle. She knew he was tired and desperate. They'd each had four fights that day, slowly eliminating the other competitors. It was simple hand-to-hand fighting with few rules except to make the opponent tap the mat in surrender. Montez had opened the fight by trying to pull off her shirt, as had another male competitor earlier in the day. Both had been defeated by a combination of rubbery fabric, her heavy sports bra, and Emilia's fist.

Emilia and Montez were both slippery with sweat. He arched his body, trying to break her chokehold or shake off the legs wrapped around his. Somehow Emilia managed to crank up the pressure on his throat while keeping his lower half pinned.

I'm a beast. A beast. The words circled inside her head. The voice of the referee and the shouts of the other cops in the gymnasium merged into an indistinguishable background roar.

Montez's hand slapped wildly, trying to find Emilia's face again. For a scary moment she thought he'd latched onto her hair, which was tightly pulled into a single braid and clamped to her head with a steel barrette, but he only succeeded in banging her head against the mat. Bloody snot gushed out of her nose and Emilia heard herself gasp for air around her mouth guard.

The crook of her elbow was a vice around his neck, cranked ever tighter by the leverage of her other hand. Montez jerked hard then rolled sideways, trying to break her hold with dead weight. Emilia held on. Her whole world was this moment, this stinking mat, this iron beast that she'd become.

But her vision was beginning to darken, there wasn't enough air and the roaring was a wave threatening to pull her under. It surged with hot hands, prying her arms apart but she was a beast, a fucking beast and she was going to—.

"Prima, let go." Her cousin Alvaro's voice cut through the wave and the roar and the mantra in her head. "You're killing him!"

Hands dragged her upright. Emilia stumbled like a drunken borracho, leg muscles quivering, and Alvaro grabbed her around the waist. The ring was full of people, including Alvaro who'd acted as her coach and Montez's friend who been in his corner all day. The police doctor and two other men she didn't recognize were bent over Montez lying prone on the mat. Beyond the ropes, at least 100 cops filled the gymnasium in Acapulco's central police building, most of them on their feet and shouting.

"You couldn't just let him tap out, prima?" Alvaro asked,

his mouth close to her ear. He shoved a wet cloth against her face as he pulled her to a corner of the ring. "You had to choke him out?"

Emilia wiped her face then spit her mouth guard into her hand. Bloody saliva clung to the bloody tape that protected both hands. She rinsed her mouth and spat into a bucket. The referee motioned her to the middle of the canvas. Montez was on his feet. Sweat ran down his bare chest and he looked dazed.

The gymnasium quieted.

"The winner of the final elimination round in the detective competition." The referee sounded more than a little stunned. He grabbed Emilia's wrist and lifted her arm over her head. "By a knockout. Cruz Encinos."

There was a smatter of applause.

And then there was silence.

By Monday, the broken nose hardly hurt at all, although Emilia still looked like she was wearing purple goggles from the two black eyes that went along with it. She hauled out her body armor vest with POLICIA stenciled across the back and closed her locker door. Alma Rosa shut her own locker and the two women stared at each other for a long moment.

"Congratulations," Alma Rosa said. She put her vest down on the bench.

Emilia nodded. "Thanks."

Alma Rosa had been her second fight on Saturday. Emilia had forced the smaller woman to tap out in less than 30 seconds. The short fight meant that Emilia was still relatively fresh by the time she came up against Montez.

"No hard feelings," Alma Rosa said. She held out her hand. "You won it fair. I never would have gotten past Montez."

Emilia took her hand then pulled the other woman into an embrace. There weren't that many female cops and even fewer good ones. Alma Rosa fell into that small group.

They picked up their vests and headed out of the locker room.

"Cruz!"

Emilia turned to see Montez charging down the hall. Alma Rosa grimaced and continued into the briefing room. At the beginning of every shift the roll was taken, assignments handed out, weapons were issued, and cops patted down to make sure they weren't carrying anything that they could use to strike a deal with gang members or cartel sicarios.

"What are you doing here, Montez?" Emilia asked. She'd learned a little about each of the other cops who'd scored high enough on the detective's exam to move to the hand-to-hand competition. Montez had a desk job in the administration building. Emilia's station in central Acapulco was foreign territory for him.

He lifted a black metal briefcase. "Courier duty," he said. "But I was hoping to run into you. What the fuck was going on with you on Saturday?"

"Sorry," Emilia said. "I didn't realize you'd tapped out."

He didn't look much the worse for wear; he was about her age, skin slightly pockmarked, short hair slicked back from a low forehead.

"I didn't tap out," Montez said, jamming himself in front of Emilia. "You were supposed to let up."

Emilia blinked in surprise. "I was just supposed to let you win?"

Montez forced Emilia up against the wall. "They're never going to give you that job. You should have let me take the competition. That way at least somebody could make detective this year. Now everybody's screwed."

"I got the highest score on the detective exam," Emilia said, her voice taut. The blood pounded in her ears. "I won the hand-to-hand. So back off. Unless you want a rematch. Right here, right now."

The door to the briefing room swung open and Sergeant Orozco stepped into the hallway, clipboard in hand.

"Cruz," he said. "Need to speak with you."

"Excuse me, *mi sargento*," Montez said and rapidly walked away.

"You're out of uniform, Cruz," Sergeant Orozco said. One of the oldest uniformed cops, he had leathery skin and dark hooded eyes.

Emilia got her breathing under control and looked down at herself. She had on the blue shirt, navy pants, and gun belt that she'd worn six days a week for nearly ten years.

"You're not going on shift looking like that," *el sargento* went on. He pointed two fingers at her face but didn't make eye contact. "Three days suspension without pay."

Emilia caught herself before she asked if that's how much he'd lost betting on Montez.

Alvaro had warned her. A uniformed cop himself, Alvaro had helped her join the force and been her guide through the early years. They'd talked about what she could expect if she tried to become a detective. Who would sabotage her efforts or take punitive action if she succeeded.

Even so, three days' worth of salary was a serious loss and she felt it like a blow to the head. What made it worse was that she hadn't expected the blow to come from Sergeant Orozco. *El sargento* had signed the supervisory recommendation required to take the detective exam. He'd even congratulated her first place score.

"On Thursday report to Lieutenant Inocente in the detectives unit," Sergeant Orozco said. "Other building. I'm sending your file over today."

Emilia nodded once. Back in the locker room she shucked off her uniform, put on her jeans and tee shirt, breathing fast through her mouth, eyes burning, refusing to cry.

Emilia presented herself at the small station on the west side of Acapulco, where the city wrapped around the lip of the bay at Playa Caleta and the divers put on their shows at La Quebrada. She didn't wear her uniform, just jeans, a black tee, and the short leather jacket that had taken six months of diligent saving to buy. Her straight dark hair was pulled into a ponytail and a careful makeup job concealed the last bruises around her eyes, which had faded to the color of premium tequila.

The sergeant behind the dispatch desk scrutinized her badge when she pressed it against the bulletproof glass. He hit the intercom. "You're Cruz?" he asked, his voice artificially metallic.

When he said her name three other uniforms came out of a room behind the sergeant's desk and stared at her through the thick glass.

It was like being a fish on the wrong side of the aquarium. "Yes," Emilia said, replacing her badge on its lanyard around her neck. "Here to see Lieutenant Inocente."

"I heard you was bigger," one of the uniforms said.

Emilia tried a wry smile.

"Down the hall," the sergeant said. "Detectives unit. His office is through the squadroom."

The heavy metal door buzzed. The latch popped and Emilia pulled the door open. She followed the sounds of arguing down the hall and into the detectives squadroom.

It wasn't a glamorous place, just a large open area with the same gray metal desks, green filing cabinets, and big wall boards covered with photographs and memos that she'd seen in other Acapulco police unit offices. But this place represented the top of her career path, the place where she'd put "Detective" in front of her name.

The place where her salary would double.

She crossed the room to the office door at the far end, getting some appraising looks from the half dozen men there. They all wore shoulder holsters and had individual computers. Emilia didn't know any of them, which wasn't surprising. Detectives maintained a very low profile to avoid being targeted by the cartels operating up and down Mexico's Pacific coast.

Lieutenant Inocente was a fit man with an expensive haircut and trim moustache. Maybe in his late thirties, he wore a starched white shirt, dress pants, and a dark tie. His office was sterile, as if he didn't plan on being there long. "Let me see your file," he said. He made an impatient give-it-here gesture across the desk.

No invitation to sit down, no welcome to the club or any other greeting.

"Sergeant Orozco sent it over on Monday," Emilia said.

Lieutenant Inocente rolled his eyes. "It'll be in Records, then," he said. "Right out of the squadroom, past the holding cells. Ask for Fabiola." He turned his attention to a file folder on his desk, effectively dismissing her.

Emilia again ran the gauntlet of appraising eyes. The uniforms at the holding cells made kissing noises as she passed. Obviously the sergeant behind the bulletproof glass had let everyone in the station know that the new detective was there.

Supplicants to the records department were kept at bay by means of a counter running the width of the room. The counter was at least a meter wide, meaning few could reach over it. Beyond the counter there were three desks. At the rear of the space, metal shelves stretched to the ceiling, all jammed with file folders of varying thicknesses.

Fabiola was twice Emilia's age, with a greying perm, glasses on a string around her neck and a mouth that twisted in disapproval when Emilia identified herself. The woman folded thick arms as she stood well back from the counter. "We don't keep personnel files here in Records," she said.

"Sergeant Orozco sent it over on Monday," Emilia pressed. "For Lieutenant Inocente."

"Maybe Lieutenant Inocente didn't need it," Fabiola said evenly.

"Could you check?" Emilia asked, ignoring the woman's implication.

Fabiola sniffed. "Come back in 15 minutes," she said.

It was the classic Mexican brush-off. Nothing would change in 15 minutes and both of them knew it.

"It looks like my file's been lost in transit somehow," Emilia said to Lieutenant Inocente ten minutes later. "If you need it today, I can go run it down. But first I'd like to talk with you about the job."

Lieutenant Inocente leaned back in his chair. As before, he hadn't invited her to sit so Emilia stayed standing in front of his desk. "Cruz," he said. "I've heard that you did everything by the book. Outstanding patrol record. Got a real nice recommendation from your sergeant. Highest grade on the exam. Won the hand-to-hand." He ran a finger over his moustache. "But the detective unit is a tight-knit group. Can't say that you're a good fit."

"Let me assure you, teniente," Emilia said. "I'm a team player. I will be giving this job my best effort."

Lieutenant Inocente slowly sat upright. "Let me put this in a way you'll understand, Cruz," he said. "Unless one of my detectives steps up and says they'll take you on as partner, you just wasted a lot of time and energy going after this job."

Emilia felt a rush of anger. "That wasn't a criteria last year," she pointed out. "Or the year before. Or any year."

"You're not last year," Lieutenant Inocente said.

He got out of his chair and walked past her into the squadroom. Emilia followed.

"This is Cruz Encinos," Lieutenant Inocente said loudly and every man in the room turned to look. "You've all heard she's the detective candidate from the ranks this year. If one of you wants to partner with her, she'll be joining the squadroom." He looked around and the words if not hung in the air. He shifted his eyes to his watch. "She'll be in Interrogation 1 for the next hour. Anybody who wants a new partner can go fix it up with her."

The painted cinderblock walls of the windowless interrogation room had once been white. Even with the door open, the ripe odor of fear and unwashed bodies thickened the air. She wondered how many brutal confessions or conveniently forgotten suspects the room had seen.

Emilia checked her watch. Thirty minutes had ticked by as she alternatively paced or stood in the doorway, staring down the hall at the holding cell guards. When one of the guards had asked what she was doing there, she'd just said "Special assignment" and shot him with her thumb and forefinger.

There was no two-way mirror so she knew Lieutenant Inocente wasn't watching, but not sitting at the battered wooden table was a matter of pride. She wasn't some criminal brought in for questioning. Besides, there was too much fury and humiliation coursing through her system to sit even if she'd wanted to.

Five minutes were left in the hour when a heavyset man came down the hall. He was in his early thirties, maybe five or six years older than her, wearing a leather jacket and holding a pair of expensive sunglasses.

He came into the room, closed the door and stuck out a beefy hand. "Rico Portillo," he said.

Emilia shook hands, glad that he didn't start a squeeze contest as many male cops did. "Emilia Cruz Encinos."

"Yeah, sure." Portillo ambled around the room, clearly uncomfortable. He stopped when the table was between him and Emilia. "I hear you're looking to become a detective," he said.

"I'd really like a shot at this," Emilia heard herself say.

"I'm a hard worker. I don't give up. You don't throw me under the bus, I won't throw you, either."

"Yeah." Portillo didn't say anything else, just fiddled with his sunglasses. After a moment he scratched his head. "The thing is," he said finally. "Right now I'm stuck with Gomez. He's dumb as wood. Dumb enough to get me killed one of these days."

"I got the highest score on the detective exam," Emilia said.

Portillo scratched his head again.

Emilia held her breath.

"You gonna turn around in three months and tell me that you're pregnant?" Portillo asked.

The air went out of Emilia all at once. "No," she said stiffly.

"You got a man?" Portillo asked. "You know, regular?"

"I'm not going to sleep with you," Emilia snapped. "If that's what you're asking."

"Hey." Portillo tossed his sunglasses on the table and raised his hands in mock surrender. "Can't blame me for trying. You're no dog, you know."

"Is that why you came in here?" Suddenly Emilia was done pushing and cajoling and fighting to get this job and everything it represented. If her only chance to make detective was teaming up with a dirty cop, she couldn't do it. "Just to see if you could get a good fuck out of it? Is that the kind of cop you are? The kind that's in it to see what they can score?"

Portillo planted his hands on the scarred tabletop. The awkwardness was gone and she wondered if it had been an act; a barrier while he assessed her. "I became a cop," he said. "Because the soul of this city is being eaten alive by the cartels and the crooks. Some of us want to save what's left."

"The soul of this city," Emilia repeated, unconvinced. "Did you make that up yourself?"

"No." Portillo reached under his jacket and pulled out a manila folder. He slapped it down on the table.

Emilia saw her name printed on the label, followed by her police identification number.

"It was in your personnel file," Portillo said. "End of your exam essay."

Acapulco Chief of Police Enrique Salazar Robelo moved down the line of those being promoted. His assistant Lieutenant Morales held out the framed certificate of the next officer. Castro Cardoso, being promoted to Captain.

Salazar shook Castro's hand. They chatted, Salazar holding Castro's handshake in both of his own for a moment of genuine congratulations. Salazar then took the heavy certificate from Morales and handed it to Castro. The official photographer snapped several pictures as the audience in the large auditorium applauded. Next, Morales handed Salazar the captain's badge and Castro ceremoniously exchanged it for his old lieutenant's badge. The captain's badge was more ornate, with Acapulco's seal of a hand holding stalks of wheat enameled in color. The photographer took a few more pictures.

Salazar stepped to the next officer being promoted. Rocha Zelaya. Promoted to lieutenant. New assignment as liaison to the head of the police union for the state of Guerrero. "Vaya con Dios," Salazar said as he extended his hand to Rocha. The union was a snake pit and Rocha would need all the help he could get.

The last officer in the line on the stage was Cruz Encinos.

"I expect it had to happen sometime," Salazar said, forcing himself to smile. "First female detective in Acapulco. Congratulations."

"Thank you," she said.

He gave her the heavy certificate. There was scattered applause as they traded her patrol officer's shield for a new detective badge.

"I won't let Acapulco down," Cruz said and held out her hand.

Salazar pressed his lips together as she waited. There was an audience. He had no choice.

Her grip matched his. Surprised, he let go first.

She was a pretty thing, looking like a recruiting poster in her dress uniform, but obviously the stories were true. The woman was a beast.

The photographer snapped away, recording the historic moment.

THE DISAPPEARED

"Badge replacement," Lieutenant Inocente said abruptly and rapped his clipboard against the frame of the doorway leading into the detectives squadroom.

Emilia Cruz Encinos looked up from her computer as *el teniente* strode to the front of the room. He was a fit man in his late thirties who was comfortable wielding power as Acapulco's chief of detectives, even if the unit only had a dozen officers. All of them were in that Monday morning, reading their email and getting ready for another day on the streets.

"You've heard the rumors," Lieutenant Inocente went on. "Entire police force is getting rebadged. Detectives are the first unit. You've got two weeks to get over to the central building, turn in your badge to the special services office, and pick up the new one." He scanned the room, clipboard extended like a sword. "Got that? Two weeks. No exceptions."

He got rumbles of assent in reply. Emilia said "Yes, *teniente*," and her partner Rico Portillo rolled his eyes at her.

Lieutenant Inocente reminded them about union dues and then what passed for a meeting was over. Emilia had been a police detective for six months and so far all of the unit's meetings had been the same. Lieutenant Inocente made an impromptu announcement or barked out orders and that was it. There was little group discussion. The detectives rarely exchanged information about the cases they worked on. The squadroom reeked of secrets and Emilia was still getting used to the smell.

Before going back into his office, Lieutenant Inocente handed out the day's assignments in the form of dispatch slips from his clipboard. Emilia watched out of the corner of her eye as he first gave out what he probably thought were the best assignments—those with the possibility of a kickback— to his favored detectives.

He handed the last dispatch slip to Rico. "Missing person for you and Cruz. Put it at the top of your case list. It's a uniform."

As *el teniente* left and the squadroom grew noisy, Emilia watched Rico's normally humorous expression tighten. "Missing since Thursday night," he said.

"Four days ago," Emilia said. "Where do we start?"

"With you." Rico flicked the dispatch slip onto Emilia's desk and began hammering at his keyboard. "Isn't that your old squad?"

Emilia hastily scanned the slip and nearly choked. The missing uniform was Alma Rosa Espinosa Lira.

"She went to the toilet and never came back. I waited for two hours." Alma Rosa's cousin Fatima was the receptionist in a doctor's office not far from the modern Santa Lucia Hospital near the big Parque Altamirano. She was in her early twenties like Alma Rosa, with the same petite frame and wavy brown hair, but wore a frightened and tearful expression which made her look twice her age.

"And you're sure no one followed her?" Emilia asked again.

Fatima blew her nose and nodded her head at the same time.

Rico huffed out his breath and glared at the nurse standing outside the small kitchen in the back of the doctor's office. They'd had to wait until Fatima could take a break. It was clear that the staff was unhappy to have two cops on the premises.

Emilia touched Fatima's hand. "Before she went to the toilet did Alma Rosa seem sleepy? Or nervous? Jumpy?"

"She was a little silly. But that's all. It was a nice place. We were having a good time."

Alma Rosa and Fatima had gone club-hopping in the popular Playa Condesa area last Thursday night; neither had to work on Friday and they were ready for some fun. They'd gone to a place offering a Ladies Night Special: free entry and 2-for-1 drinks.

"You said you had drinks with some guys at the bar." Rico came back to the small table by the microwave where the two women were sitting. "Did you get their names? What they did?"

"No." Fatima teared up again.

"Where did they go?"

"I don't know," Fatima said. "I left the bar to look for

Alma Rosa and I didn't see them again."

Emilia looked at Rico. Her heavyset partner mopped his face with a bandana and shrugged. Alma Rosa wasn't the only Missing Persons case they'd had in the past few months, and like the others, she'd seemingly vanished into thin air.

☼

"If your friend had gotten one of the new badges already," Rico said. "We'd be able to track her."

"What are you talking about?" Emilia turned to face him as Rico drove south on Avenida Ruben Figueroa toward the Playa Condesa nightclub strip. Palm trees lined the street, screening the view of car dealerships and white hi-rises, and dappling the sunlight warming the dashboard.

"The new badges have a chip in them," Rico said with a sigh at her ignorance. "So they can track us day and night. Same chips as new cars. You know, in case they get stolen."

"Making sure we don't go anywhere we're not supposed to," Emilia said slowly. She could easily believe what he was telling her. Most police officers in Mexico were assumed to be in bed with one drug cartel or another and there was always some easily-outwitted initiative going on to clean things up.

"When we're wearing the chipped badge, that is." Rico brought the car to a stop for a red light and looked at Emilia meaningfully. "But think about it. Some folks might not want to wear a locator chip all the time."

"True." Emilia waited for Rico to go on.

The light changed and the car moved forward. The noon traffic was thick with taxis, tour buses, and slowed by meandering tourists in flip flops and tie-dyed beachwear.

"Somebody's making exact copies of the new badges," Rico said. "Only they won't have the chip in them."

"Freedom of movement," Emilia said.

"Yeah."

Rico pulled into the parking lot of the nightclub. Hippo's was a fairly new place attached to one of the big hotels that often advertised in the newspaper. He cut the engine.

Emilia grabbed Rico's arm before he started to climb out of the car. "Are you going to get one of the fake badges?" she asked.

"Everybody's getting a fake one," Rico said. "You should, too."

"But you just said the chipped badges are better," Emilia pointed out. "If Alma Rosa had one she would have had it with her and we'd be able to track her."

"That's not why you need a fake badge, *chica*," Rico said.

☼

Acapulco's signature perfume was a combination of grease and salty ocean air, Emilia decided. She carried fish tacos wrapped in yesterday's newspaper and a tall glass of *agua de jamica* to a small table at their favorite outdoor *lonchería*. The place was near the water but dingy enough to stay off the tourist map. Rico juggled his double taco order and a beer as he fitted his bulk into a plastic chair.

"It's been three weeks," Rico said. "We got to close out this case."

Emilia unwrapped her tacos and squeezed a fat wedge of lime over the battered and fried fish nestled inside the tortilla. "Let's just go over it one more time," she said unhappily.

No one at Hippo's had recognized Alma Rosa from her picture. After all, she wasn't a regular and over 300 people had probably been there that Thursday night. Dozens of men had been at the bar talking to dozens of women.

No one at the nightclub knew of any date rape incidents, either. No one saw a woman being carried out that night or even leaning heavily on an escort.

No one at the nightclub looked comfortable talking to two cops.

Emilia and Rico had gone back three times to talk to different employees who worked various shifts. They went to the attached hotel to talk to the front desk, the car valets, and the bartenders in the restaurant. They scoured guest records. They talked to taxi drivers and Alma Rosa's family, friends, and fellow uniforms. They figured out the Playa Condesa bus routes and talked to late shift drivers. They followed up hotline tips, went to neighboring nightclubs, looked at security videos and called Alma Rosa's cell phone. As expected, it was out of service.

"I'm sorry," Rico said around a mouthful. "I know this was personal."

"I just keep thinking about the new badges," Emilia confessed. "I wish she'd had one."

Like the rest of the squadroom, both detectives had exchanged their badges for the new ones with locator chips in them. The new badges had a distinctive design and felt significantly heavier. Emilia was oddly reassured to think that invisible waves emanating from the badge were keeping her safe.

But wishing that Alma Rosa had gotten one of the new badges wasn't getting them anywhere. The case was a dead end, new assignments were piling up, and by the end of the meal Emilia reluctantly admitted that Rico was right. They had to retire the case.

The problem, Emilia reflected when they got back to the squadroom and she had the files spread out on her desk, was that too many Missing Persons cases looked the same. And none of them ever got solved.

Laura Carrasco Garcia didn't come home after the late shift at a grocery store. Sabina Martina Reyes disappeared while waiting for a ride in the rough Colonia Libertadores neighborhood. Guadalupe Palma went on a date with a boy no one in her family knew.

More than ten women had disappeared since Emilia had become a detective. Family grief was a thread woven through each report.

"Cruz," Lieutenant Inocente said. "Need to see you in my office."

Emilia gave an inward start. With her nose in the files

she hadn't even seen *el teniente* come out of his office. She followed him back to his desk and was surprised when he closed the door and gestured for her to sit down.

"How long have you been in the squadroom, Cruz?" he asked, leaning back in his swivel chair.

"Six months, *teniente*," Emilia answered.

"So it's about time for your first evaluation."

"I thought evaluations were annual."

"Probation period," Lieutenant Inocente said.

Emilia had never heard of any probation status. *Be careful, be careful,* played in the back of her mind. "Is this about spending too much time on the Espinosa Lira case?" she asked.

"No." Lieutenant Inocente steepled his fingers in front of his chin. "More about misunderstanding squadroom dynamics."

"I'm open to advice, *teniente*," Emilia said, keeping her tone neutral.

She wasn't sure how to defuse the situation if he made a pass at her. Just about all the detectives except Rico and Silvio, the senior detective, larded their speech with crude sexual innuendos when they bothered to speak to her at all. But so far none had given her anything she couldn't handle.

To her surprise, Lieutenant Inocente opened a desk drawer, took out two distinctively designed police badges, and laid them side-by-side on his desk. They were nearly identical. Emilia knew that one was heavier.

"Here's the advice, Cruz." Lieutenant Inocente looked at

her, obviously enjoying the moment. "A good detective is never the one who doesn't fit in. Who isn't with the program." He held up a finger and mimed cutting it off. "The one who sticks out because she doesn't do things like everybody else. You get what I mean?"

Emilia stared at the two badges. "I do."

"Good." Lieutenant Inocente swept the badges back into his desk drawer. "You bring me 1000 pesos tomorrow and you'll be fitting in fine by Friday."

Emilia went back to her desk. The air in the squadroom felt thick. It caught in her throat, as if too viscous to breathe.

"What's the matter with you?" Rico asked.

Emilia shook her head, closed down her computer, and bundled every bit of paper within reach into her deep file drawer.

Rico watched, a frown creasing his round face, and insisted on walking her out of the building. "What's the matter?" he asked again.

There was no one else in the parking lot. Emilia told him about the conversation with *el teniente*.

Rico gave a low whistle. "It was only 800 pesos last week," he said.

On Friday Lieutenant Inocente casually passed her a small package wrapped in a folded and taped manila envelope. Emilia went to drop it into the deepest drawer of her desk and realized that the files for the ten missing women were still there.

Although she knew no one was going to authorize spending any more time on the cases she couldn't help leafing through the files again. Laura Carrasco Garcia had left behind two children. Sabina Martina Reyes took a hairdressing course. Guadalupe Palma was only 16.

Alma Rosa Espinosa Lira had been her friend.

Emilia went to the supply cupboard and found an old binder. Without saying anything to anyone she loaded up the ancient copier with paper and duplicated all the relevant documents from each of the ten files. She created an organizational system and by the end of the day the binder had an entry for each missing woman and a master list of pertinent and cross-referenced details.

These women were the lost, *las perdidas*.

But maybe not forever.

Their official cases might get closed out, shunted to the side to make way for the city's unending supply of violent crime, but Emilia would keep looking, even if no one else did.

As she went to put the binder in her file drawer she caught sight of the package in its folded manila envelope. The squadroom was nearly empty. No one saw Emilia tear off the heavy paper, heft the shiny badge and replace it in the bottom of the drawer with the binder. It could stay there in Alma Rosa's new home.

A reminder of what being a detective was really all

about. And what it was not.

35

THE ARTIST

The message was delivered in the form of a *narcomanta* banner printed in black and red block letters and hung on the school's heavy iron gates. All teachers were to "donate" half of each month's salary. A teacher would be killed each week until the money was paid. But how or when the payment was to be made wasn't specified.

The banner was signed with the elaborate sword and gun shield of Los Esgrimidores. It wasn't the first time Detective Emilia Cruz Encinos had seen the logo and she was sure it wouldn't be the last. Los Esgrimidores—the Fencers—were an up-and-coming street gang in Acapulco, fighting it out in the rougher *barrios* with the long-established El Machete gang.

"We should close the school," Vice Principal José Medina Rivas said.

"There has to be something we can do." Maria Ileana Toledo Garza was the principal of the Lomas Hermosas elementary school. She was a comfortably stout woman in her early fifties with hair tucked into a tidy bun and a face made older by stress. She wore a dark pantsuit, reading glasses on a string around her neck, and brown leather pumps that badly needed polishing.

Emilia tried to keep her expression professional and calm as she sat on a bench in the small teachers' lounge. Her partner, Rico Portillo, shifted restlessly next to her. The bench was too narrow for his heavy build, although someone had tried to make it more comfortable with floral cushions.

The air smelled faintly of coffee from the machine in the corner. The room was small, with blue cinderblock walls, worn linoleum floors, and a bulletin board with notices of books to trade and teacher training sessions. The windows were covered with warped wooden blinds. Through the slats Emilia saw boys in navy shorts and white shirts playing kickball on the school parking lot.

Across from the detectives, the two administrators were obviously in conflict at a time when Emilia would have preferred to see solidarity. Medina, a bony man whose cotton collared shirt hung loose around his neck, was clearly terrified, while Señora Toledo wore an expression of grim determination.

The *narcomanta* was spread across a low table and the ends puddled on the floor. The banner wasn't some hand-painted message on a bed sheet, as so many were. This one was a professional print job on waterproofed fabric. The artistic logo looked like an elaborate Spanish family crest instead of a death threat from a gang using terror tactics to gain control of yet another Acapulco neighborhood.

Vice Principal Medina had been the one to find the banner at 6:30 a.m. that morning. Six hours later, Emilia was still surprised that the school had actually called the police and that the dispatch desk had actually slotted the assignment to the right unit. Lieutenant Inocente, Acapulco's chief of detectives, had assigned the case to Rico and Emilia with an offhand comment about not wasting too much time on it. She knew the thinking behind his words. Teachers were some of the best paid public servants, thanks to an enormously powerful national union. But there was strong enmity between that union and the more fragmented police union, making kickbacks to the police unlikely. And Lieutenant Inocente didn't like cases from freeloaders.

"In the short term, we can get patrol cars in this neighborhood to come by a few more times a day," Rico said to Señora Toledo. "We'll ask around, see if anyone saw who put up the banner. Interview your teachers, make sure this isn't an inside job. Longer term, we'll work with the Organized Crime unit to try and break the Los Esgrimidores gang. But we can't post guards and we can't shadow all of your teachers. The school needs to get some security for the gates."

"There's no money for a security guard," Señora Toledo said. "We've asked and asked the state school superintendent, but they always say there's no money."

Medina shook his head, his Adam's apple bobbing up and down as he swallowed nervously. "We should close the school," he said again. "First they target us. Next it will be the children."

"These children have nothing else," Señora Toledo said sharply. "If we close the school they'll be on the streets, ripe for gang recruitment. They'll become *halcones*, lookouts for the very thugs who are threatening them. No, I refuse to let these people deny them an education."

Emilia couldn't help but admire Señora Toledo. The woman reminded her of several teachers who had pushed Emilia to excel in school and helped her find odd jobs to scrape up money for uniforms and books. Without those teachers, Emilia knew she never would have graduated from high school, gone to a security academy, become a cop, or made detective before she was 30.

"Maria Ileana," Medina said in a low, urgent voice. "There isn't anything the police can do. If we keep the school open we're putting all of our lives in danger."

"What if we could stay?" Emilia heard herself say before Señora Toledo could answer the younger man's plea. "As surveillance. And . . . deterrence."

Señora Toledo tried not to look hopeful but the fatigue fell away from her face and she was suddenly a younger woman. "What did you have in mind?"

"Yeah," Rico said. "What did you have in mind?"

Emilia swallowed hard, trying not to think of what Lieutenant Inocente would say to this idea. She gestured at the *narcomanta*. "How many teachers have seen this and won't be back?" she asked the school administrators. "Maybe Detective Portillo and I can fill in for a few days, see who is watching the school, stay in touch with the patrol cars. If anything happens we'll be here."

"Undercover as teachers?" Rico asked, his voice thick with skepticism.

"It would let us stay around the school without calling attention to our presence," Emilia said.

"You don't have the proper qualifications," Medina protested. "We can hardly have her teaching science or math, can we? What would the union say?"

"Could you teach an art class?" Señora Toledo asked Emilia.

"Maria Ileana!" Medina exclaimed.

"José, this is more important," Señora Toledo admonished him. She turned to Emilia with an expectant look. "I'm not asking you to paint the Mona Lisa. Just supervise the children's projects."

Emilia nodded. "I could do that."

They talked a bit more about how the two detectives could integrate into the school routine, and then Emilia and Rico talked to the teachers. Most were around Emilia's age and all seemed as frightened as Medina. Rico asked some clever questions but none gave any indication of being involved.

"I think we just scared everyone even worse," Emilia said as the two detectives went back to their car. It was parked inside the school property which was surrounded by a tall wall topped with razor wire. The big iron gates were the only way in or out. "Teachers threatening to kill teachers? How likely is that, anyway?"

"Always gotta ask," Rico said. "Not just once, either."

"I'll give you a week," Lieutenant Inocente said, much

to Emilia's surprise. "Make sure Organized Crime knows what you are doing. Don't want the two of you getting in the middle of something they've got going down against Los Esgrimidores."

"We can talk to Perez over there," Rico said.

"Thanks, *teniente*," Emilia said.

"A week," Lieutenant Inocente emphasized. "After that I need you two back here. That crazy poet is bringing a protest march to Acapulco. They just announced it on the news and Chief Salazar is already calling. The same gimmick kind of march that tied up downtown Mexico City for three days. If the same thing happens here we need to be ready."

"*Oye*," Rico muttered under his breath.

Emilia knew what Lieutenant Inocente was talking about. After the murder of his son, a famous poet had led rallies in several major cities to protest the drug violence escalating throughout Mexico. Each rally had a different theme. People wore masks made of photographs of the missing, formed a human chain, or poured one drop of red colored water into a fountain for each person killed. A news pundit had claimed just the other day that the next rally would attract over a million people demanding an end to the rampant violence.

Emilia couldn't help but sympathize with the cause, but as a cop her point of view was different. Sadly, the rallies attracted a criminal element, as well as the noble-minded; and an uptick in rapes and robberies had occurred in every city that had hosted a rally. Now, apparently, it was Acapulco's turn.

Lieutenant Inocente leaned back in his chair and looked with a critical eye at the two detectives standing on the other side of his desk. "So, Portillo," he said. "What exactly will you be teaching?"

"I'll be the janitor," Rico said.

"Always knew you were cut out for higher things, Portillo," Lieutenant Inocente said.

Emilia tried not to grin.

"Gives me an excuse to get there early," Rico went on. "Open the gates. Scout around the perimeter a couple of times a day. If I can spot the lookouts for Los Esgrimidores, maybe they'll lead us to the gang leadership."

Lieutenant Inocente fingered his moustache. "What about you, Cruz? Physical education for the girls?"

"I'll be the art teacher," Emilia said. "It's a good vantage point. I can connect with all the other teachers plus watch the students, ask some questions. See if the gang has anyone inside."

Lieutenant Inocente gave a snort. "What do you know about art, Cruz?"

"We'll find out," Emilia said.

Señora Toledo introduced Emilia as a special visiting art teacher, suggesting the reason why Emilia would only be there a week was that she gave art lessons at other schools in

Acapulco as well as at Lomas Hermosas. Teachers and students, used to shortages of everything, accepted the story at face value.

Emilia had never considered herself to be particularly creative or crafty but a look through the art supply cabinet helped. There wasn't much, but the school had a pile of blank newsprint, plastic bottles of paint, colored pencils, and even poster paper in various hues.

For the most part, the children were well-behaved and happy to complete the simple projects she came up with. On the second day, she had the younger children each draw their family. When they were done she planned to tape up the pictures in the hallway outside the classroom. They'd make a big portrait gallery, Emilia promised them, and ask Señora Toledo to come for a viewing, as if it was a museum.

"How many people can be in the picture?" a little boy named Juan Pedro asked.

"As many as you want," Emilia said.

"Real people?" Juan Pedro pressed, his face pulled into a serious frown.

Emilia wondered if kids at this age had imaginary friends. "If you love them, then they are family," she said.

He accepted her words without further comment and the classroom got quiet as each student worked on their drawing. Emilia walked up and down the rows of desks, helping the children select colors and come up with ideas.

"That's Papi and Mami," said Mariana. The little girl was about 8 years old, Emilia guessed, all curly hair and wide brown eyes above her white blouse and navy skirt. She pointed to the figures one by one. "My brother Enrico, my sisters Rosalita and Flavia, and me."

Her picture showed the family standing in a row, the surprisingly realistic figures holding hands. The three girls wore the Lomas Hermosas uniform.

"That's a wonderful picture, Mariana," Emilia said. She tapped two of the figures, which were barefoot. "Why don't Papi and Enrico have any shoes on?"

"Mami says you don't need shoes in heaven," Mariana said matter-of-factly. "You walk on clouds all day and shoes would make them dirty."

It took Emilia a moment before she could reply around the sudden lump in her throat. "Your mami is a very smart lady, Mariana," she managed.

Mariana sighed as she colored in her late father's shirt. "I know."

Class was soon over and school let out with its usual clamor of departing children, all of whom were required to be picked up by a parent or older sibling instead of walking through the *barrio* alone. Emilia tidied her classroom and went down the hall to Señora Toledo's office.

She found the principal exchanging her scuffed leather pumps for equally worn cross trainers. Señora Toledo wore another dark pantsuit and a starched white blouse. She finished lacing up the sport footgear and smiled at Emilia. "You can't believe how much my feet hurt after a day in heels."

"I think I can," Emilia said with a rueful grin in return.

"I expect heels aren't very practical in your line of work, Detective."

"No, not really." Heels aside, Emilia was hard pressed to find something to wear to the school that wasn't her usual work uniform of jeans, denim jacket, and rubber-soled walking sandals. Today she'd topped black pants and flats with a simple gray pullover. Her gun was in an ankle holster.

"I'm glad you stopped by." Señora Toledo gestured Emilia into a seat by the principal's desk. "I want to apologize for José's remarks the other day. He was upset. He didn't mean to imply you weren't smart enough to teach here."

Emilia nodded her understanding. "He found the *narcomanta*. It had to have been a terrible shock."

"By taking on the art classes, you've really done him a favor," Señora Toledo said. "He won't admit it but it has been a strain on him to both teach and be vice principal. I substitute when teachers get sick but he's never given up his work in the classroom. So this is a good break for him, whether he knows it or not."

"Señor Medina is obviously very dedicated," Emilia offered.

Señora Toledo sighed. "He still wants to close the school," she said. "He has two children here and of course his first concern is for their safety. But what's worse? Living in fear or in the certain knowledge that you have failed so many children? I choose the fear. After all, it's mine. Not theirs."

"Several of these children have already lost a parent or a

sibling," Emilia said. "How are their families paying the school fees?"

Señora Toledo looked around the small office before replying. "I pay for a few," she said softly. "So they can get a good education. Grow up strong and confident. Change things before it is too late."

"I had a few teachers like you when I was growing up," Emilia confessed. "They made all the difference."

"You're making a difference, too," Señora Toledo said. "Always pay it forward. It's the only way we'll save our future."

Rico found the second *narcomanta* the next morning. Like the first, it had been hung on the school gates. He'd arrived just after 6:00 am to open the school, which meant swinging wide the iron portal so that the teachers could park inside the walls, and then relocking the gates once the children had arrived. Vice Principal Medina usually had that responsibility but had ceded it to Rico for the week. Señora Toledo always locked the gates at night as she was invariably the last to leave.

The wording of this *narcomanta* was almost identical to the other, except that the threat was doubled. Now the school could expect that two teachers would be killed each week. Like before, however, there were no instructions for passing the money to the gang.

The Los Esgrimidores logo was the same elaborate crest and the lettering was again red and black. The message had been printed on a heavy sheet of white posterboard, however, instead of waterproof fabric.

Like he had on Monday and Tuesday, Rico spent most of the day walking around the school, pretending to pull weeds from around the base of the outer walls. He identified two probable *halcones*; a nervous teen who worked at the fruit and vegetable stand on the next block, and a taxi driver who'd cruised by the school three times with an empty cab and a cell phone pressed to his ear.

When the two detectives met late on Wednesday with the school administrators, Medina was twitching with nerves and had a smudge of red ink on one shirt cuff. His hands trembled and Emilia imagined he had a difficult time holding his pen these days.

But again Señora Toledo refused to be intimidated. She did, however, accept Emilia's suggestions that they vary the school schedule and put a few of the more frightened teachers on administrative leave. She and Medina would work up a new schedule and notify parents in time for it to go into effect next week. But they would not close the school.

"I've phoned in the *placa* number for the taxi," Rico said to Emilia when they were alone in the teacher's lounge after the brief and tense meeting with the two administrators.

Señora Toledo and Medina were probably continuing their argument in the principal's office, Emilia thought. "Did you call Perez in Organized Crime?" she asked.

Rico nodded. "With any luck they'll pick up both the kid in the store and the taxi driver in a day or so."

"What about fingerprints on the *narcomantas*?" Emilia asked, although she already knew the answer. "Did the lab find anything?"

"*Oye, chica.*" Rico shook his head. "You're the queen of optimism."

They agreed that they couldn't rule out older students funneling information to gang members outside the school. Gang infiltration was a big problem for many of the schools in Acapulco, where for a few pesos, kids would provide information on teachers, the layout of the school office, and other details that could be used to rob faculty and facilities. So far Emilia hadn't seen any suspicious behavior. She'd have to redouble her efforts to find out what the kids knew. She'd also continue to ask the teachers questions.

Emilia went back to her classroom and swept the floor and tidied the art supply cabinet. She'd left it unlocked and the kids had knocked over the plastic bottles of paint and left the piles of art paper askew. They needed more paint but Emilia hardly felt like asking the principal for money for art supplies. The children would just have to make do with colored pencils.

She made a sign to go over the portrait gallery in the hall. A ceremony was planned for Friday, the last day that the detectives would be at Lomas Hermosas. Señora Toledo would view the gallery and award the little prizes Emilia had bought.

"Nice job, *chica*," Rico said as he came into the room. "Hidden talent and all that shit."

"Did I mention that blue really suits you?" Emilia replied. Rico still had on the blue coveralls that all workmen wore. The elastic waist was stretched flat by his girth.

"Of course it does," Rico said expansively. "I'm a handsome fucker."

They left together, driving through the gates just ahead of Señora Toledo who pulled to the curb. As they waited, she got out of her car in her suit and battered cross trainers, and locked the gates. She waved goodbye, returned to her car, and turned left towards home.

The third *narcomanta* was spotted with water as it hung limply from the iron gate on Friday morning. Emilia knew it had rained very late the previous night and she wondered if the Los Esgrimidores gang prowled the dark like rats looking for trash.

The elaborate logo was rendered in artistic detail and the letters were red and black. Ten children would be killed, in addition to the teachers, until the money was paid. But, like the others, the *narcomanta* omitted any delivery instructions.

Rico took the *narcomanta* into Señora Toledo's empty office. Medina passed by, early as usual, and his eyes bugged as he saw the damp poster. For a moment Emilia feared he was going to have a stroke. She led him away from the principal's office and into the teacher's lounge where she made a pot of coffee while he collected himself.

At 7:30 a.m. Medina rang the bell to signal the start of classes, despite the fact that Señora Toledo had not yet shown up for work. The principal generally came in around 6:45 a.m.

At 8:30 a.m. Emilia left her class waiting impatiently for the portrait gallery viewing and checked Señora Toledo's office. It was still empty and the lights were out. Her scuffed leather pumps were on the floor behind her desk.

Emilia ran into Medina's office. "Did you call to see where Señora Toledo is?"

"That would be your job, wouldn't it?" He thrust a list of emergency telephone numbers at her, his face white with tension.

Emilia called Señora Toledo's home and cell phones. Neither was answered. She continued down the list of numbers, finally reaching the principal's husband at his office at a building supply company. Maria Ileana had left for school at the usual time, he told Emilia in a panicky voice. His wife had told him about a school art gallery project and had been looking forward to seeing what the students had done.

Rico came into Medina's office as Emilia assured the man that they would call as soon as they had more information. When she ended the conversation, Rico made her sit down in the spare chair by Medina's desk. Medina clasped his hands together but they were shaking.

"Her car is two blocks away," Rico said. "Looks like they forced her to smash up onto the curb, then broke a window to haul her out. The seat belt was cut. I've called it in."

"Maria Ileana?" Medina gasped. "She's gone?"

"It looks like it," Rico said.

Medina abruptly started to sob, raising both hands to cover his face. He was wearing the same shirt as on Wednesday, the one with the red ink on the cuff. Or maybe it was red paint.

"You're an artist," Emilia said, barely able to breathe as a sudden weight crushed her chest. "You made the last two *narcomantas.* Using paint and poster paper from the supply cabinet. The logo and everything."

Medina sobbed wildly. Rico's jaw dropped as he looked from Emilia to the weeping vice principal.

"You wanted to scare her into closing the school," Emilia went on. "But she wouldn't."

"I just thought—." Medina choked on a sob. "She was supposed to close the school. Then no one would get hurt."

"Los Esgrimidores put up a different *narcomanta,* didn't they?" Emilia wanted to weep herself, pound the desk, turn back the clock to a different day and a different place. "With directions for giving them the money. You took it down."

"*Madre de Dios,*" Rico swore, staring at Medina.

The vice principal's sobs subsided into a guttural cough as he lifted reddened eyes to Rico. "I got here ahead of you on Wednesday and found it," Medina admitted. "I'd already made the poster so I just replaced the gang banner with it."

"And then pretended to come to work later," Rico said in disgust.

"But when she didn't close the school on Wednesday you had to up the stakes," Emilia said bitterly. "Threaten the children. She could hardly ignore that."

"I'm trying to protect these children," Medina said. "Don't you see that?"

"Was today the deadline?" Emilia asked. "Did you tell her?"

"She was supposed to close the school." Medina stood up, tears still streaming down his gaunt face as he clenched his fists. "No one could pay what they are asking. But she wouldn't close the school so I had to convince her. Frighten her. There was still time for her to change her mind."

"Apparently not," Rico said.

The line was long and the sun blazed but Emilia waited patiently along with everyone else. For the most part the crowd was silent, although now and then she heard a whispered conversation, a wail of grief, or the sound of someone crying softly. Even journalists whispered into their microphones as if reluctant to report too aggressively.

True to the prediction, at least a million people were there. Acapulco's main artery, the broad Costera Miguel Alemán boulevard, had become a pedestrian walkway, effectively bottling up the city.

The event had started at noon. Poetry was read and speeches made. Prayers dedicated to the thousands who remained missing. Pleas made to *el presidente* for a solution to the violence. And then the lines formed.

When Emilia finally made it to the canopy at the front of the line, the man behind the makeshift desk gave her a form to sign. She scribbled her name and was given a ticket and piece of printer paper on which was typed in bold black letters the phrase ***¿Dónde Están?*** Following his instructions, she wrote "Maria Ileana Toledo, Acapulco" below the letters, along with last Friday's date, and folded the paper in half lengthwise. The man let her know where she should go next.

Emilia gathered up her items and followed another line of people at least half a mile along the boulevard before finding a sign for the section marked on her ticket. She'd driven the Costera Miguel Alemán hundreds of times, yet now—lined with people and full of questions—it was unrecognizable.

The rally organizer for that section checked her ticket. Emilia was led to an imaginary square in the road, as if the avenue overlooking the ocean had become an invisible chessboard. Emilia gazed around. Every chess player had a story, every chess piece held the same question.

Emilia put the scuffed leather pumps down on the tarmac near a pair of men's loafers.

The woman arranging the loafers gave Emilia a weepy smile. "My Hector," she said with a nod at the loafers. She lifted her chin at the pumps. "Your mother?"

Emilia shook her head, surprised to find herself dry-eyed. "A friend," she answered.

She pointed the toes of the pumps toward the ocean, in the same direction as the other thousands of ownerless shoes. The folded paper with Maria Ileana Toledo's name and the anguished cry of *Where Are They?* was slipped into the right shoe so that it was positioned the same as the papers in all the other pairs of shoes. The bold question could be clearly seen. Emilia wished she'd written the principal's name in bigger letters.

The rally organizer shepherded her along as more people came into the section to set down their loved ones' shoes on the road. Emilia lost herself in the crowd swirling toward a vantage point above the beach at Playa Hornitos. The going was slow as people continually stopped to take pictures.

The road wasn't a chessboard, Emilia thought, so much as it was a cemetery. A cemetery of shoes, each pair transformed by grief into a headstone bearing the name of someone who was lost, and a question that had yet to be answered.

The headstones were sandals and sneakers and work boots and soccer cleats and bedroom slippers and platform heels and the shoes of school children worn from playing kickball and tag. They were all sizes and colors; some new, some old. The only thing they had in common was their missing owners.

Emilia snapped a picture with her cell phone, capturing

the graveyard bordering the most beautiful bay in the world. The scuffed leather pumps were lost amid so many other pairs of shoes.

She made her way out of the crowds, poetry from the rally circling in her head, an invisible weight again crushing her chest. *Dónde están, dónde están?* She was a cop, she should be able to answer such a simple question.

A salty breeze from the ocean freshened the air. It smelled like tears.

There were no clouds under her feet as Emilia kept walking, only the hot tarmac.

THE DATE

Omar Montez Serrat had a low forehead but it was offset by short wavy hair, straight eyebrows, and warm brown eyes. He was better looking in street clothes than in his police uniform, Emilia Cruz Encinos decided. She liked his choice of striped shirt, slim jeans, and suede shoes.

"Look," Montez said. "I really just wanted to say that I know I acted like an asshole after you won the hand-to-hand and got the detective job. I'm sorry."

Emilia nodded, knowing that he'd been working up to the apology. "Thanks," she said and gave a little wave at the scene in front of them. "But you didn't need to bring me all the way here to say that."

Their corner of the Mercury Club in Acapulco's popular Playa Guitarrón neighborhood was quiet enough to talk, although the sofa they were sitting on vibrated gently from the DJ's choice of music blasting from the dance floor below. They were on the second floor of the club, which was fashioned as a wide circular balcony, with private alcoves cut into the wall and the center open to the dance floor below. From the balcony railing they could see the nightclub's two parallel bars, each one running the length of a side wall, as well as the circular dance floor filled with gyrating bodies. A galaxy-themed laser show swung silvery beams across the otherwise dark and cavernous space. They'd spent a moment by the railing before being escorted to an alcove decorated with a plush sofa and indigo walls patterned with mirrored stars.

Emilia hadn't been there before but the Mercury Club was well known for its moody décor, famous DJs, and well-heeled clientele. The secluded alcoves were prime nightclub real estate and had to be reserved days ahead. It was an impressive first date, if that's what this was.

"I wanted to make a big gesture so you'd know I was serious," Montez said. He gently touched Emilia's nose with the tip of a finger. "After all, I broke your nose."

Emilia felt herself flush and was glad it was too dark for him to see. "I choked you out," she said. "I'm sorry, too. I never meant for that to happen."

Montez moved his hand to hers as it rested on her thigh. "Can we put it behind us?" he asked. "Just have a good time tonight?"

"I'd like that," Emilia said. She felt loose-limbed as she nestled against velvet and sipped her rum and cola. Maybe it was the drink or maybe it was the club's ambiance. Or the look in Montez's eyes. The way his thumb stroked the inside of her leg.

"We were rolling around together on that mat for quite awhile," Montez said. "You're hard to forget."

"That was the plan," Emilia heard herself say.

Montez grinned and crooked an arm around Emilia's neck. She stiffed momentarily, not liking the possessive gesture. Montez lowered his arm to her shoulder and Emilia relaxed. He lifted his eyebrows at her and leaned in. She met him halfway and enjoyed the sensation of his lips meeting hers. He tasted slightly sweet from the rum in both of their drinks.

Emilia felt his mouth curve into a smile as they kissed. She couldn't help smiling, too. Montez wasn't anything like what she'd expected. Not that she'd ever expected him, of all people, to ask her out. It was even more surprising when she considered that he'd really put himself out there, tracking her down to the detectives squadroom in his uniform, hat in hand, to ask if he could speak to her in private. Emilia had led him out of the squadroom and into the parking lot behind the police station and then nearly fainted when he asked if they could get together for a drink.

Montez had put aside a lot of pride to do that; he'd been the runner-up to her in the race to make detective last year. She knew a lot of cops still made jokes about his loss. She'd been impressed and not a little flattered that he'd face down all the buzz just to ask her out. So she'd accepted. The Mercury Club had been his suggestion.

Montez released her from the kiss but kept an arm around her shoulders. Emilia was wearing dark jeans and a halter top and his body was warm against hers.

"That was worth a chokehold," Montez said.

They laughed at each other. Emilia barely heard the music or saw the laser show twinkling beyond the archway to their alcove. Montez tugged Emilia close and kissed her again.

She felt herself flush all over this time. Montez was a

great kisser and it had been too long since anyone had treated her to a royal night out like this. She was pretty sure if he asked her to go home with him she'd say yes.

They finished their drinks and walked down the stairs to the dance floor. Montez wasn't as good a dancer as he was a kisser, but made up for it by staying close, keeping his torso pressed against hers. The light show flashed his face in and out of focus. As Emilia swayed to the music her police badge on its lanyard bounced against her breastbone but stayed hidden under her top. Her gun in its ankle holster was heavy but secure.

The Mercury Club was living up to its reputation. The DJ's music was lively and the laser show pulsed silver light. On both sides of the big club, the bartenders did a synchronized juggling routine with liquor bottles to the applause of their patrons.

Montez kept his arm around Emilia as they left the dance floor and headed back to their alcove for what she anticipated would be another round of rum and groping. He let her go ahead up the stairs and she'd climbed the first few when three shots rang out, fired in rapid succession from the direction of the nightclub's entrance.

"What do you think that was?" Montez asked. "Thunder?"

Five men ran past the base of the wide staircase. All

carried assault rifles and wore military-style balaclavas that masked their faces. One additionally held a large lumpy sack. Emilia shoved past Montez and ran down the stairs in time to see the man shake open the sack. Five objects rolled out onto the dance floor. Dirty volleyballs, Emilia thought blankly.

Bile rose in her throat as Emilia realized what the objects were. A woman on the dance floor stumbled as her heel snagged on human hair. Her dance partner caught her before she fell. They both looked down and recoiled in fright.

"One for one!" the man with the sack yelled. He and his cohorts raised their rifles and fired into the ceiling. This time there was no mistaking the sound. The dance floor erupted into screams and chaos. People surged toward the back of the nightclub, leaving the severed heads where they lay in the center of the dance floor. The music blared and the light show kept going, illuminating the gruesome scene with stars and comets.

The masked men let off a third volley of shots and then backed away. They kept their rifles pointed at the people huddled on the edges of the dance floor or cowering by the two long bars, daring anyone to make a move. No one did. The men fired again into the ceiling then turned and ran laughing back to the club's entrance.

Emilia shrank into the shadows as they passed. Suddenly the men were gone and Montez was next to her. "What the fuck just happened here?" he exclaimed.

"The main door's their chokepoint," Emilia said urgently. "We can catch them."

"We?" Montez asked incredulously. "We're not going out there."

"We're cops," Emilia stated.

"Off duty," Montez said.

Emilia blinked at him before it registered. As a detective, she was never off duty and was required to carry her badge and gun at all times. Montez was a uniform, however, and his weapon was issued to him before every shift.

"Call it in," Emilia said. She hauled up the hem of her jeans and pulled out her gun.

"What the hell?" Montez asked angrily.

"Call it in. Now." More shots sounded. Emilia flinched as she cautiously leaned forward to see around the curve of the stairway. People were hunched against the walls and she sensed rather than saw a commotion beyond the press of bodies.

Montez jerked her back into the shadows and gave her a shake. "What are you trying to do? Show me up?"

Emilia didn't bother to answer him. She broke away and moved toward the club's entrance, holding her gun with both hands.

The main door to the Mercury Club was open. Emilia halted just inside, and assessed the situation. A few meters on the other side of the door, two of the club's bouncers lay unmoving on the parking lot. The distinctive *burrrrp* of an assault rifle cut through the music still filtering out from the dance floor and someone in the parking lot screamed. Emilia could see three of the masked men moving around the side of the parking lot, the assault rifles softened by darkness into deadly shadows. A truck came around the last row of cars.

As the three men sprinted for the truck, Emilia bolted out of the doorway and made for the closest parked car. She moved fast but not quietly enough. The last man turned and fired, the arc of bullets following the sweep of his gaze. Emilia flung herself down behind the parked car and curled into a ball as it rocked with the impact. Glass sprayed, metal clanged, and the air filled with the bite of gunsmoke.

The thundering buzz of the assault rifle stopped. Emilia raised her head just enough to see over the hood of the destroyed car.

The truck had stopped. One of the masked men flung open the passenger side door. Another started to climb into the truck bed. The man who'd fired at Emilia was still several steps away from the vehicle.

The adrenaline surged but Emilia stayed low, leveled the sights on her automatic, and squeezed off the rounds. Time slowed into a crystal clear zone of simple motion. She heard herself breathe, just the way she always did on the police range when they practiced shooting in high pressure environments. Her finger stayed relaxed on the trigger and her shoulders absorbed the recoil.

And then the truck tires ground against tarmac, the bubble popped, and everything was fast again. The truck surged forward, spewing gravel and wild shots from the man who'd managed to vault himself into the truck bed. The man by the passenger side fell against the open door. A hand emerged from the truck cab and pulled him in. The car shielding Emilia bled glass and transmission fluid.

She stood up and kept firing until the truck careened out of the parking lot.

The third man was on his back on the pavement. Emilia ran over to him and kicked the assault rifle away from his hand. The left side of his chest was bloody.

Emilia squatted down and ripped off his balaclava. She didn't recognize him; he was just some *macho*. He stared up at her defiantly but his breathing was hoarse and bubbly.

"Who are you?" Emilia asked. "Whose heads are those?"

"*Puta*," he ridiculed her in a ragged whisper.

Footsteps sounded behind Emilia. She turned to see Montez. He gave her a shove that sent her sprawling, and knelt by the wounded man.

"Tell me who you are or you'll die right here," Montez snarled, his face close to the other man's.

The man grinned. "I die and my brother will kill you."

Emilia rolled and sat up, her face raw from the scrape against the pavement. Montez jammed his knee into the man's bloody shirt and pressed his weight into the gunshot wounds. The wounded man's face contorted in a soundless scream.

"Who are you?" Montez yelled.

"My brother," the man on the ground wheezed.

"Yeah?" Montez rocked back and forth, grinding weight against the wounds. "Who's your brother? Who the fuck are you?"

Blood stained the pavement underneath the man. "*Siempre* Esgrimidores," he whispered.

Fencers Forever. Emilia scrabbled forward on her hands and knees. "Maria Ileana Toledo," she screamed into the gang member's face. "Where is she? Señora Toledo from the Lomas Hermosas school. Where is she?"

His eyes were wide with pain but glassy and sightless. Blood trickled out of the man's mouth.

Montez stood up and grimaced at the bloodstain on his pant leg. "He's dead."

"No!" Emilia looked from the gang member to Montez and back again. Sirens sounded as she started the resuscitation routine.

"He didn't make it." Perez from Organized Crime was a short, wiry man. His eyes flickered around the hospital waiting room as he closed the door to the emergency wing of the hospital. He went over to the coffee vending machine in the small space that had been set aside for the police. His fingers rubbed against each other with small, fluttery movements as he considered the machine's options.

"Did he say anything?" Emilia asked.

"Nothing about your person of interest," Perez said over his shoulder. He chucked coins into the slot.

"Maria Ileana Toledo," Emilia supplied.

Montez was there, too, although he and Emilia had

barely spoken as they waited to hear the status of the man she'd shot and then brought back to life as he bled on the parking lot. Rico Portillo, Emilia's partner, had come to the hospital as well. She'd given Rico a private rundown of the evening in the hospital lobby while Perez was still in the emergency room with the wounded man. Once they'd come into the waiting room Montez had shaken hands with the older detective but then retreated, obviously wary of Rico's imposing girth and the thunderous look on the detective's face.

Perez extracted a paper cup from the machine, walked over to Emilia and Rico, and the scent of scorched coffee wafted through the room.

Emilia and Rico had run into Perez before. He was Organized Crime's liaison officer and ran any joint operation that the undercover Organized Crime unit mounted with other elements of the Acapulco police force. The man always wore an expensive suit and seemed totally unaware of his nervous mannerisms even as the fingers of his free hand fluttered.

"The only thing we got out of him," Perez said. "Was some gibberish about his brother. Then his eyeballs rolled and that was it."

"Said the same thing to me," Montez said. He replaced Perez in front of the vending machine.

"He said his brother would kill you," Emilia said, fighting to keep the anger and resentment out of her voice. If Montez hadn't tried to be the belated hero, they could have patched up the guy and interrogated him. They could have discovered what happened to those who'd disappeared after running afoul of Los Esgrimidores, like Maria Ileana Toledo, the principal of an elementary school who had refused to either pay protection money to Los Esgrimidores or to close the school. She'd been kidnapped by the gang and never found. The school had closed.

"He also admitted to me that they were Los Esgrimidores." Montez got a cup of coffee out of the machine.

"That wasn't an admission," Emilia said hotly. The image of Montez pressing the life out of the man rose up. "That was a dying man's battle cry."

Rico pressed a warning hand against Emilia's arm. "So we got any ID on this guy?" he asked Perez.

"We know that the leader of Los Esgrimidores, Felix Gutierrez, has a younger brother," Perez said. He paused to gulp down his black coffee.

"Gutierrez is the one they call La Espalda, isn't he?" Montez asked, with a glance at Emilia and Rico that implied he already knew the answer.

"Yes." Perez walked to a trash can by the closed door with fast, jerky steps and threw away his empty paper cup.

"You think this guy is the younger brother?" Rico asked.

"It's likely," Perez said. "Word on the street is that the little brother has been leading the fight against El Machete."

"They shouted 'one for one' when they threw the heads on the dance floor," Emilia said. "Does that mean anything?"

"Five members of Los Esgrimidores were ambushed last

weekend," Montez said.

Perez's fingers stopped their flurry for a moment. "That's right," the Organized Crime cop said. "How did you know?"

"When I'm on the street, I listen." Montez casually threw his coffee cup into the trash, too.

Emilia didn't know whether to laugh or cry. Montez rode a desk in the central administration building, pushing paper and making courier runs between the various police stations. He didn't do street work, just listened at keyholes.

"This was show-off time," Perez said. His eyes skittered around; to the closed door, then to the curtained window and then over to the other door leading to the hospital's emergency wing. "Little brother retaliates, kills five El Machete gang members. Takes the heads so there is no mistaking who they are, and shows them off in the most popular place in town. The intent was to make a big, scary public splash. Show off their revenge killings. Instead their number two got pasted and another couple of guys take a few shots, besides. Los Esgrimidores is going to have to retrench."

"So what do we do now?" Emilia asked.

Perez's eyes slid past Emilia and landed on Montez. "It was a good takedown," Perez said to the younger cop. "Organized Crime will handle it from here."

Emilia felt her fists clench and she swayed, suddenly light-headed. It was over? She'd shot a man and he'd died and she could have died, too.

Montez walked out with Perez.

Suddenly Rico was grabbing at her. The next thing Emilia knew, she was sitting in a plastic hospital chair with her head between her knees. Rico said something but she couldn't really hear him. The worn linoleum under the chair swayed to the tune of the static in her head. The room still stank of scorched coffee.

A week passed. On Friday, Emilia was locking up her desk and getting ready to leave when Montez appeared in the detectives squadroom.

He wasn't in uniform this time, but looked like a fashion spread in a dark suit and a black collared shirt worn open at the throat. His black loafers were buffed to a shine. He far outclassed Emilia in her jeans, tee shirt, and denim jacket.

The image of him that night in the parking lot of the Mercury Club, pressing the life out of the Los Esgrimidores gang member, blanked out all other thoughts for a moment. She forced it away and nodded when Montez asked if they could talk. She felt Rico's eyes on her back as she led Montez out of the squadroom. They went down the hall and out the back door by the holding cells.

"I thought you should be the first to know," Montez said. He smiled at her, the same slow grin illuminated by the laser show at the Mercury Club. Only this time they were standing in a parking lot and gritty twilight fell like a haze between them.

"Know what?" Emilia asked. She hitched up the strap of her shoulder bag.

"We got Gutierrez. La Espalda." Montez spread his feet apart with a little swagger step. "Organized Crime staked out a dozen churches after the mother claimed the brother's body from the hospital morgue."

"Churches," Emilia said. "Gutierrez showed up for the funeral?"

Montez nodded. "Yesterday evening."

Emilia's pulse soared. This was his way of making amends. She'd be able to talk to Gutierrez, ask her questions about Maria Ileana Toledo. Montez was a decent guy, after all. "Where is he now?" she asked. "Can I see him?"

"He's dead," Montez said as if surprised at her lack of understanding.

"Dead?"

"Him and all the other pallbearers." Montez laughed. "Coffin didn't look too good when the shooting stopped, either. We literally cut the top off Los Esgrimidores."

Emilia felt the blood rush to her head and then slowly recede. "We?" she asked.

Montez deliberately adjusted his suit jacket so she could see that he was wearing a gun in a shoulder holster under his left arm. "You're looking at the newest detective assigned to Organized Crime."

Emilia looked at him blankly.

Montez spread his hands. "What Perez wants, Perez gets.

Said he wanted me to join the unit. Next thing I know, I've got a new assignment, a new badge, and detective rank."

"Well." Emilia dredged up a smile. "Congratulations. I know that's what you wanted."

"I'll be working undercover," Montez said. "I guess you know what that means."

"Nice suits." Emilia kept the smile frozen in place. "Like Perez."

"I can't see you again," Montez said. "I'm undercover. You're open. It's too big of a risk for both of us."

He moved closer, intent and serious, as if both of their hearts were breaking. Emilia caught herself before she laughed in his face.

"Are you going to be okay?" Montez asked.

"Done before we got started," Emilia murmured.

Montez pulled Emilia to him. She didn't resist. Best to just get it over with rather than make a scene.

It wasn't as good a kiss as before and he knew it, but she wasn't prepared for him to yank back and snap to attention.

"Congratulations, Montez," Rico said from behind her. "Organized Crime is a good unit."

Emilia turned as Rico ambled over to Montez and stuck out his hand. The two men shook. Rico ignored Emilia's glare.

"Thanks, Portillo," Montez said. He nodded at Emilia. "I've got to go."

"I understand," she said. "Good luck."

"You, too." Montez dug some keys out of his pocket,

nodded to Rico, and walked off.

Emilia swung around to her partner as soon as Montez was out of earshot. "Were you spying on me?"

"No," Rico said, a knowing grin plastered over his round face. "Not spying. Eavesdropping. Different."

"You should be ashamed of yourself."

"Nah." Rico ran a hand though his hair. "He's a *pendejo*. You weren't going to hook up with him."

"Sometimes this job sucks," Emilia said morosely.

"Come on, *chica*." Rico put an arm around Emilia's shoulder and swung her towards his car. "My mother's made *tamales* for my brother's birthday. Everybody will be there. My brother and his wife and kids. Both my sisters and their families. Five minutes in a house of screaming kids and you'll be glad you're single."

Emilia sighed.

"Both Carmela and Lola will be there, too," Rico continued, naming his two ex-wives. The three were improbably close, with Rico swearing that he still loved them both. But he'd cheerfully admitted to Emilia one night on a stakeout that his marriages had foundered because he always put the job first. Any third marriage would be no different, but he'd enjoy it while it lasted and still love her after the divorce. "Carmela's got a new man and nobody's going to like him. There's bound to be some excitement. You know, fighting over me. Scaring the shit out of him."

"So what are you offering?" Emilia asked as they strolled through the darkening parking lot. "Dinner and a show?"

Rico chuckled. "Exactly."

"I'm only coming to help out Carmela," Emilia decided as Rico beeped open the doors of his car. "Her new fellow deserves a chance."

"He won't be better than me," Rico scoffed.

Emilia settled into the passenger seat. For a while she'd let go of all of it; Montez, the cases no one would ever solve, the way the job could get inside and twist her heart until she bled as much as the dying.

"No, he won't be better than you," Emilia said to Rico. "So few are."

THE CLIFF

"It's against Mexican law," Emilia said.

"Driving a car?" the *gringo* asked skeptically.

"Just what is your relationship to the owners of this car and their driver?" Emilia asked. The man sitting next to her desk had yellow hair and a starched blue shirt and the impatient confidence all *norteamericanos* seemed to have.

"The Hudsons come to Acapulco every few months." He pulled out a business card. "I manage the hotel where they stay."

Emilia took the card. Kurt Rucker, General Manager, Palacio Réal Hotel, Punta Diamante, Acapulco.

The Palacio Réal was one of the most exclusive and luxurious hotels in Acapulco, an architectural marvel clinging to the cliffs above the Punta Diamante on the southeastern edge of the city. Even the card was rich, with embossed printing and the hotel logo in the corner.

"Let me explain," Emilia said. She carefully laid the card next to the arrest file on her desk and tried to look unimpressed as she settled back in her desk chair. "A Mexican citizen may not drive a vehicle that carries a foreign license plate without the foreign owners of the vehicle being in it."

"So the problem was that the owners weren't in the car," Rucker said.

"Yes," Emilia said. "Señor Ruiz was alone in the

vehicle."

"The Hudsons drive down to Mexico several times a year." Rucker leaned toward her and one immaculate sleeve bumped the nameplate reading Detective Emilia Cruz Encinos. There were initials embroidered on his shirt cuff. Emilia resisted a sudden silly urge to run a finger over the stitching.

"They always hire Ruiz when they come," he went on. "They travel all over and he does errands alone. There's never had any trouble before. Monterrey, Mexico City, Guadalajara."

"Well, señor." Emilia moved her nameplate. "Here in Acapulco we enforce the law."

"Of course." His Spanish was excellent. "So how do the Hudsons get their car back?"

From across the squad room, Emilia saw Lieutenant Inocente watching her from the doorway to his office. *El teniente* nodded curtly at her then started talking to another detective. It was late afternoon and almost all the detectives were there making calls, writing up reports, joking and arguing.

Emilia opened the file and scanned the report of the arrest of Alejandro Ruiz Garcia, charged with illegally operating a vehicle with foreign *placas*. Three days ago he'd been arrested in front of the main branch of Banamex Bank. Bailed out by a cousin the next day. Ruiz had been driving a white Suburban owned by Harry and Lois Hudson of Flagstaff, Arizona. The vehicle was now sitting in the impound yard behind the police station. The keys were in Emilia's purse.

"Why are you here instead of the Hudsons?" she asked.

"They returned to the United States," Rucker said. "Before they left they asked me to help get the car back."

"They left Mexico?" Emilia didn't know why she should be so surprised. What was one car more or less to rich *norteamericanos*?

"They flew. Said it was a family emergency."

Emilia closed the file. "Señor, in order for the Hudsons to regain possession of their car they must present proof of ownership."

"Of course." Rucker passed a paper across the desk. "Here is their title to the vehicle."

It was a copy of an official-looking document. Emilia knew enough English to pick out words like name and number and address but it didn't matter. The document was meaningless under Mexican law. She handed it back with a sigh. "Señor, they need to provide the history of the vehicle, including all sales transactions and verification of taxes paid every year of the car's life."

"What?" His eyes widened in disbelief.

They were the color of the ocean far beyond the cliffs at La Quebrada.

Emilia had never seen eyes like that and it took her a moment to realize he expected an answer and another moment to untangle her tongue. "After six months, if they have not produced the necessary documentation, the vehicle becomes the property of the state."

The disbelief drained out of Rucker's face as he realized she wasn't joking. He exhaled sharply, as if he had the lungs of a swimmer, and his gaze traveled around the squad room, taking in the gray metal desks, ancient filing cabinets, and walls covered in posters, notices, and photographs from ongoing investigations. Most of the detectives were in casual clothes; those who'd been outside much of the day had shirts stained with sweat at the underarms and neck. All of them wore hip or shoulder holsters. Emilia wondered if Rucker realized that she was the only woman there.

El teniente went into his office and closed the door.

"There's a complicating factor," Rucker said to Emilia. "The Hudsons' cell phone is out of service. I was hoping that you could give me the contact information for their driver. He might have another number for them."

"I would have to check with my superior before giving out that sort of information," Emilia said primly.

"I'd appreciate it if you would and then call me." Rucker stood and held out his hand. "Thank you very much, Detective Cruz."

"You're welcome." Emilia stood up, too, and shook his hand. His grip was dry and strong.

Rucker smiled at her, a wide smile that lit his face and made the blue-green eyes sparkle. His teeth were perfectly straight and white. He could have been a toothpaste ad, the kind with the government subtitle "Cleanliness is Healthy" written on the bottom for poor people who needed to know why to buy soap and shampoo.

Emilia smiled back, caught, knowing this was the wrong place and the wrong time and the wrong man but unable to stop smiling at this *gringo* whose world of wealth and leisure was light years away from the barrio she came from. She wished she was wearing something nicer than her work uniform of jeans, tee shirt and the Spanish walking sandals that had cost two months' salary. Her gun was in a belt holster and her straight black hair was scraped back into its usual ponytail.

"*Oye!*"

Emilia gave a start and dropped Rucker's hand. Her partner Rico loomed over her desk.

"You're done here," Rico said to Rucker, jerking his chin in Emilia's direction, his leather jacket falling open to reveal his gun. "She's got a man."

Emilia felt her face flush with embarrassment and anger, but before she could say a word, Rucker held out his hand to Rico. "Kurt Rucker. Nice to meet you."

The bustling squad room was suddenly silent. Lieutenant Inocente opened the door to his office and stood in the entrance again.

Disconcerted, Rico shook hands. The handshake held for a fraction too long. Emilia watched Rico's round face tighten. He let go first.

Kurt Rucker nodded at Emilia and walked out of the squad room. The noise level went back to normal.

"Ricardo Portillo, you're a *pendejo*," Emilia hissed at Rico.

"That *gringo* has a grip like the bite of a horse," Rico said in surprise, flexing his hand painfully.

"Don't be lying and saying I've got a man unless I ask you to," Emilia whispered hotly and slammed herself into her chair.

"Stay with your own kind, *chica*," Rico warned.

"You're not my mother." Emilia jerked her chair around to face her computer, effectively ending the conversation. Rico made a snorting noise as he went back to his own desk.

Emilia typed in her password and checked her inbox. A review by the Secretariat de Gobernación of drug cartel activities across Mexico. A report of a robbery in Acapulco's poorest neighborhood that would probably never be investigated. Notice of a reward for a child kidnapped in Ixtapa who was almost certainly dead by now.

Her phone rang. It was the desk sergeant saying that a Señor Rooker wished to see her. Emilia avoided Rico's eye as she said, yes, the sergeant could let el señor pass into the detectives' area.

A minute later Rucker was standing by her desk, sweat beaded on his forehead. The starched collar of his shirt was damp.

"There's a head," he said breathlessly. "Someone's head in a bucket on the hood of my car."

The bucket was light blue plastic with a metal handle and red handgrip, one of millions sold in mercados across Mexico. The head was that of Alejandro Ruiz Garcia, the recently arrested and released driver. There were burn marks around the mouth and inside the ears.

"*Madre de Dios*," Rico said and crossed himself.

Beheadings and torture were the signature signs of a drug cartel hit. Emilia had seen death before, but rarely anything this grisly. The blood smelled sickly sweet in the warm evening air. She choked down bile and tears at the same time.

The crime scene technician eased a small piece of paper from the mouth. "'The small one cannot wait long,'" he read aloud.

Emilia looked at Kurt Rucker who shook his head unhappily. "It doesn't mean anything to me," he said.

The manner of death meant that the army was there as well as a swarm of police, all of them asking questions and scaring bystanders. Kurt Rucker's dark green SUV was parked in an hourly lot about two blocks from the police station. Although the lot was surrounded by a concrete wall and there was only one way in or out, both panicked attendants claimed to have seen nothing. Across the street, a busy sidewalk café served *taquitos* and *empanadas* and Jarritos cola but no one there had seen anything, either.

After an hour of conflicting orders from the army captain and the lead crime scene technician, the head and bucket were dispatched to the morgue. Kurt Rucker's SUV was towed to the vehicle lab to be dusted for prints and the parking lot was closed off with yellow PROHIBIDO EL PASO tape. As each owner of the cars remaining in the lot returned, their vehicle would be inspected for bloodstains and other clues that the car had transported the bucket. Emilia knew that was a forlorn effort. Some cartel thug had walked or driven into the lot, deliberately placed the bucket on Kurt Rucker's vehicle, and left immediately.

They brought Rucker back to the police station and Rico took the hotel manager's statement. It was well after midnight before Lieutenant Inocente let them wrap it up.

"Señor Rucker, this was obviously a mistake," Lieutenant Inocente said, sounding tired but less abrupt than usual. "But stay in Acapulco. We may be calling you again." *El teniente* gestured at Emilia in the offhand way he had of giving her orders while seeming to ignore her at the same time. "Take him back to the Palacio Réal and then go home."

Lieutenant Inocente went into his office and Emilia gathered up her purse and jacket. Rico's eyes narrowed. "This is just orders from *el teniente*," he warned Rucker.

Emilia led the way through the back of the police station. The discovery of the head and the search for the body meant that more police than just the normal skeleton night crew were there. Both uniformed and plainclothes officers yawned and talked and drank coffee, vibrating with the gut-popping combination of dread, excitement, and adrenaline that an obvious cartel crime always provoked. As usual, Emilia got a few catcalls as they passed the holding cell guards and as usual she smiled and pretended to shoot them with her thumb and forefinger.

"Look," Rucker said. "I can take a taxi back to the hotel."

"Don't get me in trouble with Lieutenant Inocente," Emilia said and pushed open the door to the impound yard. "You'd be robbed in two minutes trying to get a taxi in this neighborhood."

She unlocked the white Suburban and they got in.

"Is this . . . ?" Rucker asked.

"The investigating detective gets to drive a confiscated car until the case is resolved," Emilia said.

Rucker didn't reply.

At the exit Emilia leaned out the driver's side window to show her identification to the impound yard guard. The big gate swung open.

The police station was located in the old part of Acapulco on the western side of the bay. Emilia drove through small streets, past the old cement buildings and billboards advertising Herdez vegetables and Tía Rosa snacks, getting the feel of the Suburban. She'd barely had a chance to drive it since being tossed the keys by Lieutenant Inocente the day Ruiz was arrested. "*Finalmente*," he'd said, which Emilia took to mean she'd finally landed a case with fringe benefits.

The streets widened as they turned onto la Costura, the city's main artery, and cruised through the center of Acapulco. Despite the late hour, traffic was heavy. The evening had just started at clubs like Carlos and Charlie's and

Señor Frog's. The Malecón beachfront vibrated with dance music. This was where the younger *turistas* came and shopped and spent money and saved the rest of them.

"I didn't even know him," Rucker said.

"I know." Emilia had listened as Rico pushed Rucker hard. But Rucker's story had been consistent. He'd managed the Palacio Réal for nearly two years and had no contact with Mexican police during that time. He knew Ruiz only in the context of the man being a seasonal employee of frequent hotel guests. As *el teniente* had said, it had to have been a mistake. Maybe the head was intended for the owner of a different car in the lot.

"So what's with your partner?" Rucker asked. "Is he your bodyguard as well?"

Emilia shrugged. "You're a *gringo*."

"So I can't talk to you?"

"Look," Emilia said, torn between loyalty and attraction. "Two years ago I was the uniform cop who got the highest score on the detective exam. Even broke my nose in the hand-to-hand test. But they didn't want a woman so they made up a new rule. I couldn't become a detective unless somebody who already was a detective agreed to take me on as partner." She looked away from the road to meet Rucker's eyes. "Rico was the only one who stepped forward."

Rucker's gaze was disconcerting. "So you owe him?"

Emilia flushed. "Not like that," she said.

They didn't talk again as they left the lights of the city behind. The Suburban was heavy and unwieldy, laboring to climb the rises and wallowing in the declines. Emilia was glad for the quiet; all her energy was devoted to managing the vehicle.

It was at least a dozen miles to Punta Diamante, the picturesque spit of land southeast of the city. Along the way, la Costura became the coastal highway called the Carretera Escénica, winding high up the side of the mountain that guarded the most scenic bay in the world. The road was a ribbon of tarmac carved from the face of the cliff, two dark lanes without guardrails or a safety net. Far below, on Rucker's side, the bay twinkled and shimmered under the night sky. A few cars passed heading toward Acapulco but for the most part they were alone on the road with nothing to spoil the dramatic scene of mountain curves and glittering ocean.

"You know the hotel entrance?" Rucker asked.

"Yes." The Palacio Réal was part of an exclusive gated community built into the cliff face below the highway. From the huge privada gate a steeply pitched cobbled road led down to the water, linking private villas, a luxury condominium building, and the Palacio Réal hotel complex.

Emilia slowed to turn right into the gate entrance. Headlights blinked on in back of them and her rearview mirror suddenly filled with glare.

"Where's the army checkpoint?" Rucker asked sharply.

All the major hotel entrances were guarded by the army. But tonight there was no big green vehicle, no soldiers milling around, nothing.

"*Jesu Cristo*," Emilia gasped. She stamped on the accelerator, the engine groaned and the Suburban strained to pick up speed.

The headlights in her mirror suddenly grew large. As the Suburban passed the deserted *privada* gate a salvo of gunfire tore the night and something hit the back bumper with a dull thud. The heavy vehicle shuddered and slewed to the right.

Emilia broke out into a cold sweat as she fought the wheel, trying to keep the vehicle on the high mountain road. The tires on the right side lost traction along the cliff edge. Time stopped for a day and a year before the lethargic vehicle responded and rumbled toward the center of the road and then the rear window exploded, spraying glass inward. Emilia and Rucker both instinctively ducked as shards rained down but Emilia kept the accelerator pressed to the floor.

The Suburban lurched around a slight bend. The glare in her rearview was refracted for a moment and Emilia saw the vehicle behind them clearly. It was a small pickup, with at least four men braced in the bed. They all carried long guns.

"We can't outrun them," Rucker said.

"I know."

"Brake and turn it."

"*Madre de Dios*." Before she gave herself time to think, Emilia hit the parking brake and swung the wheel to the left.

The small truck shot by as the Suburban screamed into the oncoming lane, tires chewing the tarmac, engine protesting. The mountainside loomed out of the inky darkness so fast Emilia felt the vehicle start to claw its way upwards. But momentum and gravity won out and the vehicle continued to spin.

The landscape was lost in a dizzying blur. Like a hand racing too fast around a clock face, they were pointed toward Acapulco in the right lane, then at the center of the road, then at the other lane, then straight at the cliff edge. Far below, white lines of waves rolled gently toward the sand, hypnotic and teasing.

Suddenly Rucker's hands were on Emilia's helping to straighten the wheel. He reached across her body and released the parking brake lever. The Suburban shuddered and surged forward, wind coming through the shot-out rear window like a monsoon. Together they wrestled the vehicle back into the right lane.

They hugged the mountain as the Suburban plunged down the highway back toward Acapulco. Emilia nearly lost control several times as the heavy vehicle was propelled by its own weight. Next to her, Rucker kept a lookout for the truck but didn't see it. "Maybe they tried the same thing and went over the cliff," he said.

"No." Emilia saw the welcome glow of the city and turned off the headlights in a vain attempt to hide. "They know where you live. They'll just wait for you to come back."

The night was very black. Once they hit town Emilia wove through the narrow barrio streets she knew so well until she was sure they hadn't been followed. The neighborhoods were deserted. She parked the Suburban in an alley, killed the engine, and found she couldn't breathe.

"You did good out there," Rucker said, his voice like a safe haven in the darkness.

Emilia nodded and sucked in air. Her face was wet.

"You okay?" Rucker asked.

"What do these people want from you?" Emilia's voice sounded harsher than she intended. She wiped her tears away with the back of her hand. "Did you lie to Rico?"

"A better question might be who knew you were taking me to the Palacio Réal," Rucker said.

Emilia blinked at him as fear surged into her throat yet again.

Rucker folded his arms and stared out the windshield. The neighborhood was nothing more than trash and cement and cardboard roofs that would last only until the next rainy season. "We've got twenty of these cars at the hotel for hauling luggage and guests," he said. "Fully loaded, none of them handle this bad."

"What are you talking about?"

"This car is hauling something."

"*Jesu Cristo*, we could be sitting on a ton of cocaine," Emilia managed. Everything connected. "Somebody wants it and you've been the only link to the car since Ruiz got arrested and the Hudsons left."

"Know anybody who can take a car apart?" Rucker asked.

Emilia swallowed hard. "Yes."

☼

Three hours later they were staring at five million green *Estados Unidos* dollars piled on the floor in her uncle Ernesto's auto repair shop. The rear body panels of the Suburban were off, exposing the ingenious system welded into the car frame to accommodate brick-sized packages. Even the four-wheel drive mechanism had been cannibalized to create more hidden hauling capacity.

"Money in, cocaine out," Emilia said. "The Hudsons are mules."

Rucker fingered one of the dollar bills, his forehead furrowed with thought. The hotel manager had worked side-by-side with Tío Ernesto as if he repaired cars in a greasy garage every day. His beautifully starched shirt had been cast aside, revealing a white singlet undershirt and muscular arms. Both the white undershirt and his khaki pants were now as dirty and oil-spotted as Tío Ernesto's coveralls.

"These are brand new bills," he said.

"So?" Emilia got him a glass of water from the big jug of Electropura purified water. Tío Ernesto had gone to the one-bedroom apartment over the shop to tell Tía Lourdes to make them all some breakfast.

"A couple of years ago they changed the design of American money." Rucker spread several bills on the tool bench. "Made the image bigger. Added a tint. New watermarks." He took a swallow of water. "But these are the old design."

"What are you saying?" Emilia ran her finger over the

crisp paper. "It's counterfeit?"

"Only way to find out is with one of those bank scanners."

"Ruiz was arrested in front of the Banamex," Emilia said slowly.

"I know the manager at Citibank," Rucker said. "He'll scan it for us and won't say anything, either."

He leaned against the tool bench as he studied the money, his *norteamericano* confidence undimmed despite the setting. Oil filters and alternator belts were stacked haphazardly on shelves, plastic jugs of used oil filled a corner, a garbage can overflowed and at least one rat had scurried away when a bleary-eyed Tío Ernesto opened the door and waved in the Suburban. Then Emilia had felt as if the garage was a sanctuary. Now she wasn't so sure she'd done the right thing.

"I grew up here," she blurted.

Rucker looked up at her, eyebrows raised above the blue-green eyes.

"My father died when I was little," Emilia heard herself say. "Tío Ernesto is his brother. My mother and I came to live here with him and Tía Lourdes and their two boys. Six people in a one bedroom apartment."

Rucker didn't react.

"My cousins taught me how to fight. How to keep away from the cartel *sicarios* and the other men who wanted girls to sell to the *turistas*." She was challenging him for no good reason, throwing the *barrio's* harshness at him as if it was his fault "My mother wasn't right after my father died. She didn't work and we didn't have any money. Most weekends I sold candy or fruit at the highway toll booths. Until my cousin Alvaro helped me to join the police. That's when my mother and I moved into our own house. Being a detective is good money but not for a place like the Palacio Réal."

Rucker pushed himself away from the tool bench, took out his wallet, and slowly and deliberately folded several of the *Estados Unidos* bills inside. He replaced the wallet in his hip pocket, peeled off the stained singlet and picked up his dress shirt. Emilia watched the muscles of his chest and abdomen flex as he put on the shirt and buttoned it.

"By the time I was six I was the best milker in the family," Rucker said evenly. "On a dairy farm everybody milks the cows twice a day. Cows don't care if you're sick. If it's freezing cold. They still need to be milked."

He rolled up the shirt sleeves, hiding the monogram. "When I was 18 I'd milked enough cows to last me a lifetime and I enlisted in the Marine Corps. Fought in a couple of places. When I got out I went to college. Studied hotel and restaurant management so I could spend time in places as far from that farm as I could get. Sent my parents a couple of tickets last year to come visit but they'd rather stay with the cows."

They looked at each other. An awkward silence was broken by the sound of footsteps and rattling pans overhead.

Rucker gestured at the dismantled Suburban. "Well, Detective, the bank will open in about an hour. How do we want to get there?"

"I think that you could call me Emilia," she said.

☼

They took an anonymous green and white *libre* taxi to the bank. Rucker's friend was the manager, a polished Spaniard who swallowed a comment about Rucker's appearance as Emilia displayed her detective badge.

Ten minutes later, the currency scanner confirmed Rucker's theory. The money was counterfeit.

"Excellent fakes," the bank manager said. "And given that there are just a handful of currency scanners in Acapulco for this high a denomination of American bill, quite a clever scheme."

"You never saw us," Emilia said. "You never saw these bills."

☼

By the time they were back in the garage, Emilia had made up her mind. She didn't tell Rucker until they were alone in Tía Lourdes's kitchen. She could tell he didn't like the idea. But he didn't have anything better to suggest.

"If we don't let them find the car and the money they're never going to leave you alone," Emilia insisted.

"How are you going to explain losing a car?"

Emilia rubbed her eyes. Last night's adrenaline had

ebbed, leaving her tired and shaky. "We won't lose it. They want the money, not the car. We can pull a spark plug to make sure they leave it and pick it up later."

"We're letting them win," Rucker said.

"We're making sure you stay alive." Emilia opened her purse and pulled out a pen, paper, and her cell phone. "We'll copy the serial numbers from the bills to trace the money. That way we might even catch who's passing it."

Rucker slumped in his chair and nodded. "All right."

She dialed Rico.

"You sure you trust him?" Rucker asked abruptly.

Emilia heard Rico's voice grunt "*Bueno*?" For a wild moment she wondered if Rucker was right. But if she couldn't trust Rico then there was no one to trust at all. Kurt Rucker looked away as she told Rico what had happened and what they needed him to do.

They reassembled the Suburban and its counterfeit load and abandoned it on a little rocky outcropping along the Carretera Escénica about two miles past the gate to the Palacio Réal.

Rucker broke the spark plug just as Rico drove up at the wheel of an old *libre* taxi. Emilia and Rucker jumped in the back and then they were gone.

The taxi was one of thousands and attracted no attention as it puttered up to the *privada* gate. The army checkpoint was in place. The sergeant studied Kurt Rucker's identification before gesturing to his corporal to open the gate.

The brakes on the old taxi strained against the steep pitch of the road as they passed the carefully manicured foliage of the luxury villas. All of the villas cost tens of millions of pesos, Emilia knew. Several Hollywood stars had homes there, as did many of Mexico's entertainment and business elite. Every meter down the road was a step further away from Kurt Rucker.

His arrival at the Palacio Réal confirmed the distance. As Rucker climbed out of the taxi in his stained khakis and rumpled shirt, a platoon of uniformed doorman and bellhops swarmed around him. More staff materialized, all smartly dressed, the women in the hotel's signature blue print dresses, the men in stone-colored slacks and coordinating blue shirts. *Señor Rooker, we were so worried . . . Señor Rooker, we had a problem with . . . Señor Rooker, you need to call . . .*

Rucker stepped away from the throng for a moment and met Emilia's eyes. She smiled tightly. He gave her a little salute and went into the hotel.

Through the glass doors Emilia could see a wide lobby open to the ocean. People in clean white clothes carried cool drinks as they walked by the grand piano.

"Not your kind, *chica,*" Rico said. He put the car in gear and they started the long painful drive up the steep road to the highway.

☼

The next morning Emilia and Rico went back to the Suburban. It had been dismantled and the money taken out. The body panels seemed to have been replaced in a hurry. The rear fenders were hung at an awkward angle and all four of the doors were jammed closed. Rico raised the hood and put in a new spark plug.

Emilia looked past the vehicle to the bay. Kurt Rucker was in his hotel right below where she was standing. Maybe having his breakfast, his clothes cleaned and pressed by the hotel staff. Maybe on the telephone, giving orders. He'd already forgotten the terrifying moments when their hands were locked together on the steering wheel. Forgotten telling her about working on a farm.

Forgotten her.

The sound of crying lifted on the warm salty breeze. Emilia walked back to the Suburban and nearly had a stroke.

A small boy about five years old was huddled on the floor of the back seat, partially concealed by a dirty blanket. Both of his hands were swathed in bloody bandages.

"Rico!" Emilia shouted and somehow wrenched open the rear passenger door. The child cringed, his face contorted in fear and pain.

Emilia eased herself onto the floor of the Suburban next to him. Shards of glass were everywhere. The child lifted his hands in their bloodstained bandages as if to ward her off. Emilia realized with a jolt that his thumbs were missing. "It's all right," she breathed. "I'm going to take you home."

"Madre de Dios." Rico leaned over the front seat. "It's the child from Ixtapa. The kidnapping from Ixtapa."

The boy nodded and his face crumpled. "I want to go home," he sobbed. "Mama."

Emilia pulled him close. She rocked him as he cried, her own body shaking. "The small one cannot wait long," she whispered to Rico. "We paid the ransom."

It was a rare meeting of all the detectives. They stood in a knot in the middle of the squad room, joking in low voices as they waited for *el teniente* to come out of his office and tell them why he'd called the meeting.

Emilia talked with those few who'd gotten used to having her around. It had been two weeks since she'd driven the Suburban back to the impound yard and claimed that hooligans had shot out the rear window while she was investigating a robbery in a bad neighborhood. Lieutenant Inocente had signed the requisition for new glass without comment.

Since then the investigation into Ruiz's death had more or less stalled out. Attempts to find out which army sergeant was working the night she and Rucker were going to the Palacio Réal had led nowhere. None of the money had turned up, but ransom money almost never did.

She and Rucker had spoken once. A call to tell him about

the kidnapping. She'd stammered through an account of finding the child, Rucker's voice making her feel unaccountably foolish and unsettled, then abruptly ended the conversation.

Lieutenant Inocente walked out of his office and the detectives fell silent. *El teniente* held up a clipboard. "I have a letter to read."

He cleared his throat and peered at the clipboard. "'This letter of commendation goes to Detectives Ricardo Portillo and Emilia Cruz Encinos for the recovery of Bernardo Estragon Morelos de Gama. The child was rescued by the detectives and will make a full recovery from his ordeal. The Morelos de Gama family extends heartfelt gratitude and this reward to these two outstanding Acapulco detectives.'"

The detectives applauded. Emilia managed a weak smile as Lieutenant Inocente handed her a thick envelope. Rico's face wreathed into a huge grin as he accepted his own.

There were congratulations all around and some beers to share before the squad room settled down and the rest of the day went on. Rico locked his envelope in his desk drawer and Emilia did the same; less important items than cold cash frequently disappeared in the squad room.

Emilia spent the rest of the morning wondering how much money was in the envelope. She would buy her mother a new dress. They could both get their hair done in a real salon. Splurge on a meal in a restaurant. She and Rico exchanged little smiles of anticipation.

At noon Lieutenant Inocente dropped the keys to Kurt

Rucker's SUV on her desk. "Call him and tell him to pick it up today. The paperwork's ready." *El teniente*'s gaze included both Emilia and Rico. "You should open the reward."

He'd said it like an order. Both Emilia and Rico unlocked their drawers and took out the envelopes. Emilia opened hers and took out 500 very familiar Estados Unidos dollars with small images of a norteamericano president.

Her heart beat so fast that for a moment her vision blurred.

"Congratulations," *el teniente* said.

"Thank you," she managed.

Rico's face was set in a blank smile. Lieutenant Inocente nodded at both of them and went into his office.

Without changing expression, Rico stared at Emilia until his meaning was clear. She made a conscious effort to relax her face muscles and breathe. Rico finally gave a barely imperceptible nod and replaced his money in the drawer.

Emilia put her money in her pocket, got out Kurt Rucker's business card and left a message with the hotel that he should pick up his car at the police station.

He came a few hours later. Two weeks hadn't changed him, although this time he was wearing jeans and a black polo shirt and looked faintly more tan.

"You need to sign some paperwork," Emilia said before Rucker even had a chance to say hello. She stood up with his keys in her hand. "Please follow me."

She felt Rico's eyes on her as she led Rucker out of the

squad room and down the hallway. They went past the holding cell guards and Emilia smiled and shot them with her thumb and forefinger. At the impound counter she asked the secretary for the paperwork. They waited, Emilia painfully aware of Rucker standing calmly beside her.

The secretary finished her cigarette, lounged over to a file cabinet, licked her fingers and pulled a file out of a drawer. She studied the contents as if she'd never seen a typed form before. Eventually she replaced the file in the drawer, licked her fingers again and found another.

His was the fourth one. The secretary thumbed through it, left it on her desk, and disappeared through a doorway into an interior office.

"She probably hasn't worked here long," Rucker observed. It was the only thing he'd said since coming.

"Sixteen years," Emilia said.

The secretary came back holding a light blue plastic bucket with a metal handle and a red handgrip, one of millions sold in mercados across Mexico. She thrust it at Rucker along with the paperwork to sign. "You're to take this," she said.

Emilia felt the message like a physical blow. Rucker signed the paperwork. It was duly stamped with the authority of the police, the city of Acapulco, the police officers' union, the state of Guerrero, and the self-importance of the secretary. Finally everything was in order and Rucker was handed the holy form giving him permission to take his car off police property.

Emilia pushed open the door to the impound yard. The late afternoon heat pressed against the rows of cars. The yard appeared deserted. Rucker stopped walking and turned to Emilia.

She handed him the reward envelope.

He put down the bucket and opened the envelope. Emilia saw surprise cross his face at the sight of the bills. "Where'd you get this?" he asked.

"From *el teniente*." Emilia heard the bitterness in her voice. "Our reward for solving the kidnapping of that poor child. The 'small one.'"

"He called off the army that night, didn't he?" Rucker asked, fiddling with the envelope. "He's a dirty cop, Emilia. In on that kidnapping. This is to let you know he's thinks he can scare you. Or buy you. You have to report him."

"Report him?" Emilia laughed, a short bark that sounded more like a sob. "Who would I report him to? The army officers he paid off? The chief of police who chose him for the job? The union official who gets a take? The mayor who appointed all of them? Which of them would protect me?"

"They can't all be dirty," Rucker said and handed back the envelope.

"I'm the one holding the fake money," Emilia snapped and jammed the envelope into the back pocket of her jeans. "The chica detective nobody wanted in the first place."

Rucker stared at her for a moment as the truth of what she was saying sank in. "There's got to be something."

"It'll be like it always is," Emilia said harshly. "A few

clean cops, a few dirty ones. Some get rich and some get dead and you hope the cartels don't win in the end."

Rucker touched her cheek. "Are you scared?"

Emilia's throat was suddenly tight and her eyes burned. She shrugged.

"Have dinner with me," Rucker said. "Come down to the hotel and we'll sit by the beach. We'll figure something out."

The sun was low in the sky, sending streaks of light across the roofs of the parked cars. Emilia tried to imagine herself explaining a relationship with a *gringo* to her mother. To Rico. To her cousins.

"There's nothing to figure out," she said, forcing the words out around the lump in her throat. "It's like they always say. 'Poor Mexico. So far from God, so close to the United States.'"

There was a movement at the open door to the shed by the impound yard gate. A uniformed cop came out and stood where he could see them.

Rucker looked around. Emilia followed his gaze to his green SUV in the second row of vehicles. He looked back at her. "I guess I should go."

Emilia nodded.

"Stay safe," he said.

"No promises," Emilia replied.

Rucker's face tensed, then he turned and walked away. Emilia watched him. The light blue plastic bucket dangled from his fingertips as he passed between the rows of cars.

She went back inside and into the women's public

restroom. The latch on the door of the farthest stall was blurry as she struggled to lock it.

Emilia gulped air and fought the urge to sob. She yanked the envelope out of her pocket. She would rip those *maldita* bills unto bits, flush them down the toilet, and deny she'd ever seen them.

She opened the envelope and her tears gave way to an unexpected gasp of laughter.

Alongside the counterfeit money was a fancy laminated coupon for a free drink at the Palacio Réal's Pasodoble Bar.

EL Fin

The Cliff story grew into the first Detective Emilia Cruz novel, **CLIFF DIVER**. Get it wherever books are sold.

"Consistently exciting" – Kirkus Reviews

"A thrilling series" – National Public Radio

BONUS! Turn the page for the first two chapters of Carmen's political thriller **THE HIDDEN LIGHT OF MEXICO CITY,** longlisted for the 2020 Millennium Book Award.

THE HIDDEN LIGHT OF MEXICO CITY

Chapter 1

"The next step is to follow the money," said Eduardo "Eddo" Cortez Castillo.

"That's quite some story, Eduardo." Across the table, César Bernal Paz gave his head a bemused shake as if collusion between Mexico's Minister of Public Security and the elusive leader of the country's most notorious drug cartel was a remote and amusing concept.

"There's enough evidence for a warrant." Eddo felt his scalp prickle under the brown hair he kept as short as a general's.

"Really," Bernal Paz said absently. He sliced into the *arrachera* steak on his plate and put a morsel into his mouth.

Eddo reached inside his Brooks Brothers suit jacket, took out a folded document from the inner pocket, and placed it on the starched tablecloth between the two place settings.

Bernal Paz eyed the heavy ivory paper and embossed black border. "*Secreto*, eh?"

The two men were in a private corner of arguably the most exclusive restaurant in Mexico City. The Sanborn's restaurant on the top of the historic Casa de Azulejos near the huge Zocalo square was the lunchtime bastion of Mexico's power elite. The staff was unfailingly discreet, the atmosphere was dim and elegant, and more deals and careers were made and broken there than in the president's office in Los Pinos.

"The warrant is for the central bank to report all of Hugo's financial transactions for the past year, including money transferred out of the country," Eddo said quietly.

Bernal Paz blinked in astonishment, his steak momentarily forgotten. "No. No." He hastily wiped his lips with his napkin. "Honestly, Eduardo. I can see now why you've been telling me all this. But as senior governor, I cannot let the central bank become involved in some petty rivalry between you and your superior."

"This is not personal, Don César," Eddo said in all truth. "I hold Hugo de la Madrid Acosta in very high regard. I hope this investigation proves to be nothing. But we need the truth."

"Yes, of course." Bernal Paz raised white eyebrows. He was an aristocratic man who clung to the elegant manners and rigid societal rules of those few who controlled the country's money and had complete faith in their right to do so. He wore a fitted Italian pinstripe suit and a discreet designer tie with matching pocket square. "But you have to see it from my point of view. You are investigating your own minister. Very awkward."

"The warrant is signed by Judge Arturo Romero," Eddo countered. The problem was that the warrant was Secret. Only a handful of people knew of its existence. Mexico's legal system was so arcane that if Bernal Paz refused to comply there wasn't anybody who had the knowledge and legal authority to compel him, including the president.

"You know him. Not just for this." Bernal Paz made it a statement, not a question.

"My professor in law school."

"Yes. I recall your father saying that." The older man leaned back in his overstuffed chair. "I suppose now you'll tell me that if Judge Romero wins the presidency you're in the administration."

Eddo raised his wine glass in a mock toast. "Attorney General."

"Will you be the youngest?"

"I'm already past 40." Eddo said. "Probably not."

Bernal Paz smiled back magnanimously. "I lose track of the years, Eduardo. To me, you'll always be a boy playing *fútbol*. Running like the wind with the eyes of an angel." He wagged a finger at Eddo. "You should be on television."

Eddo nodded his acceptance of the compliment even as he indicated the document on the table. "Arturo asked that you personally oversee the warrant."

"And when he gets to be president Judge Romero will remember warmly those who were his friends before the election?" Before Eddo could reply, Bernal Paz reached out with a forefinger and slid the warrant toward Eddo's plate of salmon. "But Romero might not even get the party nomination now that Lorena's decided to run."

Eddo suppressed a grimace. Mexico's First Lady Lorena Lopez de Betancourt had tried very hard to upstage her husband ever since Fernando Betancourt had been elected president. Her latest antic was to announce that she wanted to be president when her husband's term expired.

"You don't think she'll get the nomination?" Bernal Paz polished off his steak. The older man's relief that they were no longer talking about the warrant was palpable.

"She has no financial backing." Eddo slid the warrant back to Bernal Paz's side of the table. "Can you get me the information within two weeks?"

"Really, Eduardo." Bernal Paz sounded like a stern schoolmaster speaking to a wayward pupil. "The central bank cannot be involved in dirty politics."

"Ministers of the government cannot be permitted to join the cartels." Eddo kept his voice low, although the effort was nearly killing him. He wanted to jump up and shout, make Bernal Paz see how critical it was that they have the banking records, squeeze the old man by the throat until the numbers popped out of his ears.

"All the evidence you have so far is circumstantial." Bernal Paz made a dismissive gesture with his fork. "The land his son supposedly bought from El Toro--."

"Reynoldo de la Madrid is 14 years old, Don César," Eddo interrupted. The sale of a large tract of desert land from a man using cartel boss El Toro's Christian name to one Reynoldo de la Madrid had been recorded by the town clerk of Anahuac, a small town south of Nuevo Laredo, and reported by a local cop. "Some teenager in the most expensive private Catholic school in the country, with bodyguards around him even at the Santa Fe shopping mall, is not making his own deals with cartels."

"Eduardo, you don't understand." Bernal Paz pursed his lips and pushed the warrant back across the table. "I would like the central bank to help, but getting this type of information is very difficult. It cannot be done and that is final."

"It's all on computers," he countered. "No doubt you have a good systems administrator who can get it done."

Bernal Paz frowned. "Listen to me, Eduardo. Hugo is a powerful man. If he finds out he'll bring down the bank."

"The bank is an institution," Eddo pointed out. "It will survive.

Bernal Paz shifted uncomfortably in his chair. "No. You ask too much."

"So we're too afraid to save our country?" Eddo pressed, leaning forward. "What will you leave your grandchildren? A country that's just a playground of violence for the cartels?"

"Eduardito, that's enough," Bernal Paz scolded.

The childhood nickname was a warning sign and Eddo knew it was time to give Bernal Paz some space. He sat back in his chair and signaled to the waitress. She deftly removed their plates and brought coffee.

"My father always said if I needed anything I should come to you," Eddo said after awhile. He poured some cream into his coffee and stirred it. "That's why he always kept the Marca Cortez money in the Banco de Vieja Puebla."

"Marca Cortez and Banco de Vieja Puebla go back together for more than 200 years." Bernal Paz loaded his coffee with sugar and looked at Eddo meaningfully. "This is what matters in Mexico. Family. History. Tradition. Not your silly secret warrants."

The words were thick with significance. Eddo didn't reply but again let the silence draw out, watching the older man sit impassively across the table, reproof etched on his patrician features. Bernal Paz's refusal to conduct the bank investigation had nothing to do with his fear for the central bank or even, really, of Hugo de la Madrid Acosta. No, it was Eddo's insolence in growing up and attaining a position of power over not only his elders but his peers in Mexico's highest social class, the *criollos* who could still claim a pure Spanish bloodline. Tradition meant preserving the social order and Eddo was threatening to upset it. What he was doing simply wasn't done by one of their own.

"Marca Cortez values the relationship with Banco de Vieja Puebla, of course." Eddo sipped some coffee. The caffeine hit his stomach and set it alight. "I still sit on the board of directors and Uncle Bernardo and I speak frequently."

"And Octavio oversees Marca Cortez's financial interests just the way I did when I headed the bank."

Eddo carefully centered his cup in its saucer. "I'm just a little concerned that Octavio might be, ah, how shall I say . . . distracted."

Bernal Paz frowned, the white eyebrows dipping toward

his nose.

"Three months ago a certain Senorita Vida Sandoval Arnez bore Octavio fine twin boys," Eddo continued softly. "They live in a fine new house in Cuernavaca that Octavio bought at a cost of three times his annual salary from the bank. He's a frequent visitor. Of course, it must be heartbreaking to be away from Elena and the children so much. And his duties at the bank."

Tension hung in the air, stretched by silence. "How do you know this?" Bernal Paz finally asked.

"Octavio's private life is between him and Elena," Eddo replied. "But a bank with a distracted director is not a safe place for Marca Cortez."

To the old man's credit he didn't flinch. They both knew that if Eddo recommended it, his uncle Bernardo Cortez, Marca Cortez's chairman, would move the company's money elsewhere. Banco de Vieja Puebla would collapse and the Bernal family fortunes along with it.

A muscle in Bernal Paz's jaw bunched. "How long have you been director of the Ministry of Public Security's Office of Special Investigations?"

"Over four years," Eddo said. "I was the first official sworn in after the election."

"Four years." Bernal Paz's voice trembled with anger. "In all that time you've been concealed. Lurking in the shadows. Oh, you've caught some people and made a few statements. But even when you were seeing that blonde television woman no one knew who you were."

Eddo nodded once in acknowledgment. For the year they'd dated he'd managed to stay on the periphery of Elsa's fame. She'd hated his reserve and avoidance of the limelight right up to the day they'd agreed to go their separate ways.

"This is not what your father wanted for you." Bernal Paz jabbed a finger into the air at Eddo. "You were a disappointment. He wanted you to take over Marca Cortez. To be its lifeblood the way he was. Instead you run off to that fancy *norteamericano* college. Let Romero fill your head with crazy ideas in law school and then you threw away all that education by joining up with the police. You were with scum and you've become just the same." Spittle flew from a corner of his mouth. "Never marrying, never carrying on the Cortez name. You wipe your feet on tradition, Eduardito. And now this. You're the man who lifts skirts to see the shit underneath."

Eddo pushed the warrant back to Bernal Paz's side of the table. "Two weeks. Whatever you find send to the office at Marca Cortez."

Bernal Paz snatched up the warrant and stuffed it into the inside pocket of his superbly tailored suit jacket, his face tight with suppressed fury. "I do this only because when I pray for the repose of your father's soul I can say that when his son asked for help and invoked his name I gave him the help he asked for."

Eddo nodded.

Bernal Paz pushed out his chair and stood. The man was older, more frail than when he'd entered the restaurant two hours before. Eddo stood up, too, and at that moment their status and power were equal.

"Mark my words, Eduardito." Bernal Paz's voice was so low Eddo had to strain to hear. "Hugo de la Madrid Acosta is a powerful man. He'll learn of this investigation and when he does, you're a dead man. A dead man."

Eddo met Bernal Paz's eyes. "Maybe I already am."

"Two weeks," Bernal Paz spat. "And you will not be welcome in my house again."

The old man stalked out of the restaurant, acknowledging no one although he probably knew most of the patrons.

Eddo sat down. A wave of nausea hit him and he had to lift his chin and gulp air to prevent the searing bile from coming up.

"Señor?"

The waitress in her elaborate pleated paper gown smiled at him inquiringly as she lifted away the remains of the meal. "A *postre*, señor? I could show you the dessert tray."

"No, thank you," Eddo said hoarsely. A sugar rush was the last thing he ever needed. "A brandy, please."

The waitress brought a balloon glass and Eddo sipped the brandy, listening to the hum of unspoken deals and the slick murmur of political wheels being greased. The nausea passed, leaving his body churning with tension and residual adrenaline. The exchange with Bernal Paz had been a hell of a way to end the week, especially given his lack of sleep. He was dealing with the pressure of the investigation with his usual prescription of running and working out, but it was turning him into a chronic insomniac.

At least tomorrow was Saturday, the day when he'd go to La Marquesa, the big area of scrubby parkland between Mexico City and Toluca. He'd played fútbol there every Saturday since his earliest police days.

That's when he'd run and run until he was nothing more than two feet and a pair of lungs, until he coughed blood and stank of sweat and forgot for an hour or two everything that he was and what he had to do and the people who'd get hurt along the way.

Chapter 2

Three votive candles burned in front of Our Lady of Guadalupe. There was no one else in the living room to see the tiny flames shiver in the draft as Luz de Maria Alba Mora shut the front door.

In the cheap reproduction painting, prominently displayed in a wrought iron easel on top of a weathered wood cabinet, the Virgin wore a green robe decorated with stars just like when She'd appeared to San Juan Diego in 1531. The picture was draped with rosaries, silk flowers, and a black ribbon marking the day 13 years ago when Luz's father and grandfather had been struck by a bus and the world had changed forever.

"I'm home," Luz called. She put down the backpack

containing her sketchpad and the pay-as-you-go Amigo cell phone that was just for emergencies.

"In here." Luz's mother's voice filtered through the doorless archway to the kitchen.

Luz peeled off the sweatshirt she wore over a tee shirt and jeans then found her mother behind the ironing board. More than a dozen crisp men's dress shirts hung on a clothes rack wedged between the board and the scrubbed pine kitchen table.

"*Hola, niña.*" Maria Mora was a small, plump woman with tired eyes, a ruddy complexion, and short permed hair. She set the iron on its heel as Luz stretched across the board so the two women could exchange kisses. "Was the bus ride all right? Did anyone bother you?"

"Nobody bothered me, Mama," Luz said. She'd learned how to take care of herself long ago but her mother asked the same question every time she came home. "Everything was fine and the bus even got in a little earlier than usual."

"Good, good," Maria said and took up the iron again. Her brown polyester dress was as old as the kitchen's chipped yellow and blue tiles. "The children are still at school and your sister's at the church for the ladies craft afternoon."

"Poor Father Santiago," Luz said. She turned on the single cold water tap, found the bar of naptha soap, and washed her face and hands, getting rid of the stink of diesel fuel, worn vinyl, and unwashed passengers. "I don't know how he stands all their chatter."

"They're planning the *oferta* for the Day of the Dead,"

Maria said.

"Every woman there is going to have a different plan," Luz said with a wry smile.

Maria chuckled.

Luz dug her pay envelope out of the front pocket of her jeans where it had been safe from the pickpockets that roam bus stations. She opened the jar kept on the counter for household money. Only a few pesos left this week. Working as a *muchacha planta*--a live-in housemaid--earned Luz time off every other weekend and Wednesday afternoons and paid 5000 pesos a month. It was good money but it was never quite enough.

"You keep some to do your hair," Maria said, lifting her chin at the jar even as she kept the iron moving over the cotton shirt on the board. "You should have done it the last time you were home."

"I know," Luz said. "But the weekends go by so fast." Like so many women of *mestizo* heritage--the mix of conquering Spanish and defeated *indio* that made up the majority of café-skinned Mexicans--Luz wore her hair long and permed with bangs curved into a bubble over dark brown eyes. But the perm and the bangs had grown out and lately her head was just a mass of hairpins trying to keep everything in place.

"We have to go to the *mercado*, too," Maria said. "The girls need new shoes. Those two grow out of everything."

Luz put 300 pesos for a new perm in her jeans pocket, dropped the rest of the money in the jar, and opened the cupboard to find an aspirin. The four hour bus ride from Mexico City to the small town of Soledad de Doblado on the outskirts of Veracruz was a huge descent in elevation and she had the usual headache. Of course, everyone had headaches in October when the summer rains gave way to the dry season and sinus pressure fluctuated like crazy. She washed down the aspirin with water from the *garrafon*, the big bottled water dispenser on the counter, and looked at her mother. "I saw the candles," she said leadingly.

Maria pressed the shirt cuffs, the last step in a professional ironing job. "We got some good news."

"Really?" Luz raised her eyebrows. "What sort of good news?"

Maria smiled. "You can wait," she said. "We'll sit and have some coffee and then I'll tell you all about it."

"I'll keep ironing while you make the coffee," Luz offered. The dry cleaner's bag at her mother's feet was still half full; she'd obviously gotten a late start on the 40 shirts she ironed daily for 2 pesos each. Luz took the finished shirt from her mother, hung it on the big rack, flipped a plastic shroud over it and stapled the dry cleaner's coupon to the plastic.

Puffing with exertion, Maria squeezed herself out of the corner between the rack and the ironing board. Luz swiveled her hips and slipped easily into the tight space. Rather than Maria's soft stockiness, Luz had inherited her late father's height and lithe build, along with his high cheekbones and wide mouth. She spread a new shirt over the board.

"I'll make coffee with milk the way you like it." Maria filled the coffee maker's glass carafe with water from the dispenser.

Luz felt her headache lift as her mother bustled around the small kitchen, heating milk in a battered saucepan and finding the right glasses for *café veracruzana*. Obviously a celebration was at hand. Maybe Juan Pablo had won Student of the Quarter again.

The coffeemaker gave a final gurgle as Luz finished her third shirt. She unplugged the iron and sat at the table across from her mother. Maria set a glass of coffee and hot milk in front of her and Luz sipped appreciatively.

"Your sister is pregnant," Maria said and put three heaping spoonfuls of sugar in her own glass.

Luz nearly choked on her coffee. "Lupe?"

"You only have one sister," Maria said.

"She can't be pregnant," Luz sputtered. "She's a widow with two small daughters."

Along with Luz, Lupe had left school when their father died but had been too shy to work as a *muchacha*. She'd married young and been widowed a few years later. Still shy, she crocheted placemats and bowl covers for the tourists at the handicrafts *mercado*.

"She's pregnant," Maria said. "I said I'd tell you before she got home."

"Is she sure?" Luz searched for other possibilities. "Maybe she's got the flu. Ate something that upset her stomach."

"She's sure," Maria replied. "She's already been to the clinic. They made her buy some vitamins."

Luz blinked. "That's why there wasn't anything in the money jar."

Maria nodded. "The vitamins cost almost 200 pesos."

Self-pity hit hard as Luz stared into her glass of *café veracruzana*. Lupe was pregnant and soon there would be another mouth to feed and Lupe had two beautiful children already and Luz would never have any.

"I lit the candles," Maria continued. "For her to stay healthy. Twenty-six is old to be having babies."

And 29 is ancient. Tears pricked the back of Luz's eyes as she wrestled with feelings she thought she'd crushed long ago. She'd never married and never had a child in a country where the majority of girls of her social class were mothers before their eighteenth birthday, married or not. "*Madre de Dios*," Luz said harshly. "This was your good news?"

"Babies are always good news, Luz."

"This is not the right time," Luz said. "Juan Pablo graduates from school this year. How are we going to send him to college with all the costs for a baby?"

"You know there's no money for college, Luz." Maria's voice was flat. "There never was. Your brother will get a job."

"No," Luz snapped, although she knew her mother was right. College cost a fortune, but it was one of Luz's dreams that Juan Pablo would go. He was brilliant. "We haven't scrimped and saved to put him through Colegio Santa

Catalina just so he can end up working on the docks in Veracruz."

"He'll be all right," Maria said.

"And I want Martina and Sophia to go to Santa Catalina," Luz said stubbornly. "That neighborhood school isn't teaching them anything."

"The tuition for Santa Catalina is 1800 pesos a month," Maria said. "Double for two. We can't afford to send them and you know it. They can stay where they are for 400 pesos a month. When Juan Pablo graduates and we're not paying his tuition things will be easier."

"There's no room in this house for any more people," Luz went on, unable to stop herself. Maria's bedroom was off the living room. Two other bedrooms and the only bathroom were upstairs. When she came home Luz slept on the floor in the room she'd shared with her sister when they were girls, but which was now used by Lupe and her daughters. "We're cramped enough as it is."

"Luz de Maria." Maria banged her spoon on the table. "What do you expect your sister to do? Get herself cut up by some back street butcher?"

Her mother's words stung. Luz slumped in her chair. Abortions were forbidden by the Catholic Church. And illegal in Mexico. "Of course not," she mumbled. "Does Juan Pablo know?"

"Yes. She told us both last week when she came back from the clinic."

"And Martina and Sophia?" Luz drank some more

coffee. An unhappy acceptance settled into her bones. "How is she going to tell the girls they'll be getting a new brother or sister?"

"She said heaven was sending them a new baby."

"*Madre de Dios*," Luz swore softly. "Heaven had nothing to do with this. Who's the father?"

"She won't say."

"What do you mean, she won't say?" Luz looked at her mother in irritated surprise. "Somebody has to provide for this baby, not just Lupe." *And me.*

"She won't say," Maria repeated.

"Did you ask?" Luz asked, appalled that her mother was willing to let Lupe keep such a secret. "Make her say."

Maria shook her head. "She doesn't want to."

The front door creaked. There was a rush of childish chatter and then Lupe and her daughters came into the kitchen. The little girls squealed with delight to see Tía Luz and Luz's heart gave another lurch of self pity as she hugged and kissed both of them. Martina and Sophia were 5- and 7-year-old miniatures of Lupe, short and solid and sweet tempered. They wore their school uniforms; navy jumpers and white blouses. After they climbed all over their aunt, Lupe made them go upstairs and change. They did as they were told without argument, leaving the three women alone in the kitchen.

"Mama?" Lupe's soft brown eyes flickered with nerves.

Maria nodded and poured another glass of coffee and hot milk.

"She told me," Luz said as guilt churned her stomach into slurry. She hugged her sister. "How are you?"

"I'm fine, just fine." Lupe smiled timidly. She took after Maria and was smaller and plumper than Luz. Her hair was short and permed and she wore a plain polyester skirt and blouse. She sat down with her glass and added sugar. "They do this quick little test now at the clinic."

"When are you due?" Luz asked. She went behind the ironing board again and attacked another shirt.

"May," Lupe said happily. "We can have the baptism before Juan Pablo's graduation."

"Won't that be nice," Maria said, watching Luz.

"Nice," Luz agreed, calculating swiftly. She couldn't recall anything significant happening in August. "Early May or late May?"

"May tenth." Lupe smiled. "Maybe it will be a boy this time."

And what will his name be? Mexicans took the names of both parents' fathers. Luz's own name was the combination of Alba, her paternal grandfather's name, and Mora, the name of her mother's father. The paternal name always came first and was always used, although some more progressive Mexicans were dropping the everyday use of the second name. Luz's employer Señora Vega used both names, and added the name of her husband's father as well, preceded by "de," something usually only done by upper class people.

"Who's the father, Lupe?" Luz asked.

Her question was met with silence.

It was truly the first time she could remember that Lupe had hidden anything from her and Luz was suddenly frightened. She slammed down the iron, ran around the table, and grabbed Lupe by the shoulders. "Did he rape you?"

"No, Luz." Lupe shook her head. "He's . . . it's . . . it's good."

"So you have a boyfriend?" Luz asked in surprise.

"It's nice, but it's not like that." Lupe squirmed out of Luz's grasp. "I don't want to talk about it right now."

"Why won't you tell us, Lupe?" Luz pressed.

"Luz," Maria said warningly.

"He should know first," Lupe said.

"Look, Lupe." Luz folded her arms, determined to find out what horny macho had done this to her sister. "You can't--."

"I knew you wouldn't be happy about this, Luz," Lupe cut in, her voice still soft and timid. "That's why I asked Mama to tell you. You're the one with the important job. You can draw and paint and remember what you read and make decisions. Juan Pablo's smart and good at everything. But being a mother is what I'm good at." She held up her hands in a gesture of supplication. "I've wanted another baby for so long, Luz."

Luz stared at her sister. She hadn't realized that Lupe wanted anything. Since her husband's death Lupe had seemed content with her daughters and her needlework. And Luz had her own lost dreams to cry over.

Lupe gazed back; untroubled, at peace.

"I'm glad for you," Luz managed. She bent again and hugged Lupe.

"You're the best sister in the world, Luz." Lupe hugged back hard.

"Hardly." Luz closed her eyes and felt unutterably sad.

Lupe sniffed and broke the hug. "Wouldn't trade you for another brother."

The old joke broke the tension. Luz turned back to the ironing board. Lupe got out her crochet basket and lifted out a piece of half-finished lace.

"If the new baby is a boy," Luz said, determined to sound cheerful. "Juan Pablo can teach him how to play *fútbol* and chase girls." She finished the shirt and handed it to Maria who slipped it into a plastic shroud and attached the coupon.

The three women fell into the familiar comfort of each other's company while they worked. They talked about Juan Pablo, on whom they all doted, and Luz described the latest happenings in her employer's house. There was Marisol the cook to talk about, plus Hector the chauffeur, Raul the old gardener, and of course Rosa, the harebrained other maid with whom Luz shared an attic bedroom. Señor Vega and his latest girlfriend always provided good grist for the story mill, as did Señora Vega and the society events she attended and the unbelievable clothes she wore to them. Luz talked, too, about the three Vega children who all went to the bilingual Colegio Americano, the most expensive school in Mexico City.

It was her twice-monthly unfolding of the drama of the

Vega household, those people who lived in that other world. Luz usually made it sound like a *telenovela*, but this time she knew her voice was a little flat.

Find ***THE HIDDEN LIGHT OF MEXICO CITY** wherever books are sold*.

"Riveting political drama" – Literary Fiction Review

Longlist, 2020 Millennium Book Award

You're invited

122

You're invited to stay up to date with Emilia and the team in Carmen's Mystery Ahead newsletter. Get behind-the-scenes details and must-read recommendations every other Sunday. Plus the occasional recipe from food featured in the books!

Subscribe at carmenamato.net/mystery-ahead/

About the Author

Carmen Amato turns lessons from a 30-year career with the Central Intelligence Agency into crime fiction loaded with danger and deception.

Starting with *Cliff Diver*, her award-winning Detective Emilia Cruz mystery series pits the first female police detective in Acapulco against Mexico's drug cartels, government corruption, and social inequality.

The series was awarded the Poison Cup for Outstanding Series from CrimeMasters of America in both 2019 and 2020 and has been optioned for television.

Her Galliano Club historical thriller series was inspired by her grandfather who was a deputy sheriff during Prohibition.

Originally from upstate New York, Carmen was educated there as well as in Virginia and Paris, France, while experiences in Mexico and Central America ignited her writing career.

Every other Sunday, Carmen shares her top secret(s) in the Mystery Ahead newsletter.

Subscribe at carmenamato.net

www.ingramcontent.com/pod-product-compliance
Lightning Source LLC
Chambersburg PA
CBHW020046310726
48970CB00007B/2429